"Thanks for seeing me home," Star said

"I wanted to see you home safely."

She was annoyed that Dermot still thought he was her protector. "I'm the one carrying a gun," she replied.

"Excuse me? I don't believe I came across a weapon on the dance floor."

Nearly blushing at the reminder of how close they'd danced, she said tartly, "Seriously, I'm carry-ing."

Dermot stepped toward her and slid his hands around her waist. "Where?" His thumbs hooked under the edge of her sweater and sent shivers along her flesh.

"Wrong part of the anatomy," she said, strangely breathless. "Try an ankle holster."

She knew she ought to go inside—like right this second!—but she was caught by the magic of the moment. She raised her hands and rested them lightly against Dermot's chest.

Her heart quickend. "Dermot…"

Without answering, he pulled her hard against him. Her pulse doubled as she realized he was going to kiss her.…

Dear Harlequin Intrigue Reader,

Temperatures are rising this month at Harlequin Intrigue! So whether our mesmerizing men of action are steaming up their love lives or packing heat in high-stakes situations, July's lineup is guaranteed to sizzle!

Back by popular demand is the newest branch of our Confidential series. Meet the heroes of NEW ORLEANS CONFIDENTIAL—tough undercover operatives who will stop at nothing to rid the streets of a crime ring tied to the most dangerous movers and shakers in town. *USA TODAY* bestselling author Rebecca York launches the series with *Undercover Encounter*—a darkly sensual tale about a secret agent who uses every resource at his disposal to get his former flame out alive when she goes deep undercover in the sultry French Quarter.

The highly acclaimed Gayle Wilson returns to the lineup with *Sight Unseen*. In book three of PHOENIX BROTHERHOOD, it's a race against time to prevent a powerful terrorist organization from unleashing unspeakable harm. Prepare to become entangled in *Velvet Ropes* by Patricia Rosemoor—book three in CLUB UNDERCOVER— when a clandestine investigation plunges a couple into danger….

Our sassy inline continuity SHOTGUN SALLYS ends with a bang! You won't want to miss *Lawful Engagement* by Linda O. Johnston. In Cassie Miles's newest Harlequin Intrigue title—*Protecting the Innocent*—a widow trapped in a labyrinth of evil brings out the Achilles' heel in a duplicitous man of mystery.

Delores Fossen's newest thriller is not to be missed. *Veiled Intentions* arouses searing desires when two bickering cops pose as doting fiancés in their pursuit of a deranged sniper!

Enjoy our explosive lineup this month!

Denise O'Sullivan
Senior Editor, Harlequin Intrigue

VELVET ROPES
PATRICIA ROSEMOOR

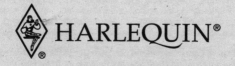

HARLEQUIN®

TORONTO • NEW YORK • LONDON
AMSTERDAM • PARIS • SYDNEY • HAMBURG
STOCKHOLM • ATHENS • TOKYO • MILAN • MADRID
PRAGUE • WARSAW • BUDAPEST • AUCKLAND

ISBN 0-373-22785-X

VELVET ROPES

Copyright © 2004 by Patricia Pinianski

This edition published by arrangement with Harlequin Books S.A.

® and TM are trademarks of the publisher. Trademarks indicated with
® are registered in the United States Patent and Trademark Office, the
Canadian Trade Marks Office and in other countries.

www.eHarlequin.com

Printed in U.S.A.

ABOUT THE AUTHOR

To research her novels, Patricia Rosemoor is willing to swim with dolphins, round up mustangs or howl with wolves—"whatever it takes to write a credible tale." She's the author of contemporary, historical and paranormal romances, but her first love has always been romantic suspense. She won both a *Romantic Times* Career Achievement Award in Series Romantic Suspense and a Reviewer's Choice Award for one of her more than thirty Intrigue novels. She's now writing erotic thrillers for Harlequin Blaze.

She would love to know what you think of this story. Write to Patricia Rosemoor at P.O. Box 578297, Chicago, IL 60657-8297 or via e-mail at Patricia@PatriciaRosemoor.com, and visit her Web site at http://PatriciaRosemoor.com.

Books by Patricia Rosemoor

HARLEQUIN INTRIGUE

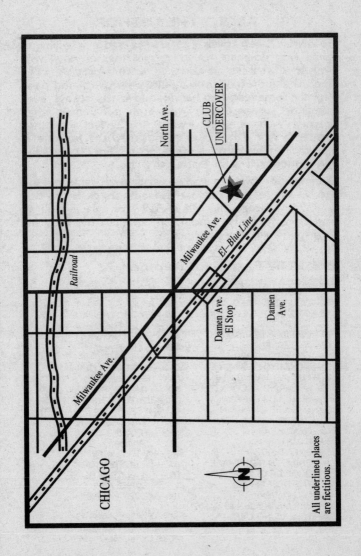

CAST OF CHARACTERS

Dermot O'Rourke—The wealthy psychiatrist has no choice but to turn to Star Jacobek and the team at Club Undercover when he's framed for murdering one of his patients.

Detective Star Jacobek—She owes Dermot big for helping her in the past, but can she prove they have a future together?

Tony Vargas—The ex-con was hung with velvet ropes from the same church Dermot had visited hours before the murder.

Frank Jacobek—Star's uncle was there for her when her father died, but is he the key to finding the real killer?

Alderman Marta Ortiz—The victim's cousin is determined that no one will look too closely into her past.

Johnny Rincon—The former gang leader let Tony take the fall for him in a robbery years ago.

Luis Zamora—The cop who used to be a gang member owed Tony Vargas big.

I would like to thank both Sergeant David Case and Officer Susan Heneghan for answering myriad questions about Chicago police officers and procedures.

Prologue

Tony Vargas slipped into the blackness of his room and leaned back against the door, hugging the laptop to him as if it could prevent his heart from exploding through his narrow chest.

Then a tic of nervous laughter spilled from him, and he flicked the switch next to the door. A small chandelier—proof that the halfway house on Chicago's south side had been a posh residence a century ago—lit the barren room with its twin beds, scarred high-boy dressers and rickety chairs. Home, such as it was, if not for long. He'd done it—he'd stolen the sanctimonious psychotherapist's computer practically from under his nose. Should be worth a couple of C-notes on the street…if not more for what he might find inside.

And more jail time if you get caught, a little voice in his head taunted him as he threw himself on the bed, opened the laptop and turned it on.

"I won't get caught," he muttered. "Not this time. This time I'm golden."

This time everything was going his way. No more days in the kitchen because he was too scrawny for harder work, no more nights being someone's date because he wasn't strong enough or mean enough to defend himself. And soon he would be free of the halfway house with enough money to get him a decent place…a car…women…

The operating system brought the computer up to speed and Tony went straight to the word-processing program, straight to a folder named Heartland. Just like the halfway house.

A no-brainer.

"Too easy, Doc," he muttered, opening the folder and finding a file on each of the dozen residents.

Eager to get the dirt on the other ex-cons living in the dump—something that could give him leverage if not cash—he nevertheless couldn't resist the file named Vargas. What had O'Rourke said about him?

No need to wonder. He opened the file and skimmed the notes about himself. Basically a shorthand transcript, these were from their last session only. *Yada, yada, yada.* Big deal. Only the final entry made Tony raise his eyebrows and curse himself for not learning to keep his mouth shut.

Then he snorted and shook his head. What did it matter what Dermot O'Rourke knew? He was bound by therapist-patient confidentiality. Kind of like that seal-of-the-confessional thing they'd had going years ago.

But he wanted to sell the laptop on the street, so getting rid of evidence against himself would be the smart thing. Wouldn't do to let someone have the goods to blackmail *him.* Before he could exit the file to delete it, however, the doorknob rattled.

Rattled himself, Tony shoved the still-running laptop out of sight under the bed. "Hey, Bingo, that you?" he called, wanting to believe his roommate had torn himself away from the television downstairs this early.

"Open the door, Tony."

Recognizing the voice, Tony cursed softly, then trying to appear as if nothing were wrong, made for the door and opened it. Far more casually than he was feeling, he asked, "Hey, what's happening?" His mouth was spitless and the words tumbled out in a rush.

"Did you think you could get away with it?" his visitor asked, pushing Tony back inside and locking the door. "Did you think I wouldn't know it was you?"

"Hey, it was a joke. I didn't mean—"

"Didn't you learn anything in that cell?"

Tony backed away nervously, gaze glued to the hands twisting a purple velvet rope like the ones holding back a crowd from a club entrance...or inside a church. He used to put velvet ropes in place outside the confessional at St. Peter's, part of his job as an altar boy.

Tightening his hands into fists so he wouldn't make the sign of the cross and betray his fear, he asked, "Wh-what are you gonna do with that thing?"

A rhetorical question.

No one had to tell him he was a dead man.

Chapter One

"Tony knows better than to try blackmail…has a death wish…" Detective Mike Norelli looked up from the transcript. "What about it, Doc?"

Dermot O'Rourke sat back in his creaky wooden chair in the pasty-green Chicago Police Department interrogation room and took in the Violent Crimes tag team assigned to Tony Vargas's murder. Norelli and his partner, Detective Jamal Walker, were as different as night and day. Middle-aged and beefy, Norelli wore a bland, dark suit, white shirt and forced smile. Younger and fitter, Walker apparently had more interest in being a snappy dresser than friendly. Both men leaned over the table toward Dermot like two vultures ready to pick at carrion.

Not that he was officially under arrest.

Not yet.

But Dermot knew how this could go down. He was no stranger to the system, and they knew that. He'd done a couple of rounds in Juvenile Detention—the last time just for physically protecting himself from a rival gang member. That experience—added to know-

ing that next time he would be treated like an adult—
had been enough to scare him straight.

If the Vargas case went bad, he wouldn't be so
lucky this time around.

"What about it?" Dermot finally echoed. "I enter
abbreviated session notes on the laptop to be more
fully written up later for my files."

"Do you always threaten your patients?" Walker
asked, pushing his dark face closer.

Dermot didn't so much as flinch. "I don't like your
innuendo or your tone, Detective. Maybe I should call
my lawyer?"

He was bluffing, of course—he didn't trust lawyers
any more than he did cops. Too much bad experience.
But he figured the threat sounded good.

"Do you have reason to need a lawyer?"

"Whoa, whoa, whoa," Norelli said with a cheesy
smile, apparently playing good cop. "We just need to
know what you know about Tony Vargas. No accu-
sations here."

Maybe not, but there certainly were implications
Dermot didn't like. They hadn't asked him to come
down to Area 4 simply because he'd counseled Tony,
the little thief. They could have interviewed him at
Heartland House where he donated his time to help
ex-cons get back on their feet.

He hadn't wanted to go back to the old neighborhood—ever—but he'd gone to Heartland as a favor
to Father Padilla, the priest who'd helped him out of
the gang wars and set him on the road to a decent
life. He'd figured one night a week in the Pilsen
neighborhood wouldn't kill him.

Hah!

If he was arrested and found guilty...

"Be specific, then," Dermot gritted out. "What do you need to know?"

"The reference to blackmail in your notes on the laptop. Who was Tony's target?"

"I wouldn't know. He never told me."

"And if he had, *would* you tell us?" Norelli asked.

Dermot didn't respond to the baiting. One wrong word and he could be inside.

"You're not a priest no more," Walker said. "No seal of the confessional here."

He never really had been a priest, Dermot thought, though he'd worn the cloth for a short time—a huge mistake on his part. He never had what it took. Not the calling, anyway. But guilt had proved to be a great motivator.

"No, only therapist-patient privilege," he said so much more calmly than he felt. "But in this case, with my patient dead, I would tell you what I knew *if* I knew anything that would help catch his killer."

"Unless you don't want the killer caught."

"*If* this was even a murder. How do you know it wasn't suicide?"

Dermot knew he was reaching. Tony had never seemed the type, but if he'd gotten himself into enough hot water that he was desperate...

"Wollensky walked into the room and found him swinging from the chandelier," Norelli said. "He went downstairs, called 9-1-1, then waited for the uniforms to go back into the room. They figured suicide, but when one of 'em picked up the overturned chair Vargas'd been standing on, the officer spotted the laptop. Guys in halfway houses don't have computers unless they steal 'em. So the officer grabs the laptop, thinking he'll run the serial number and see who it belongs to, but it's still running. And what does he see but your note about blackmail.''

"So come on,'' Walker joined in. "What was that secret you and Tony shared?''

Dermot started. "Secret?'' Nothing in his session notes with Tony indicated they'd shared a secret.

"Don't play dumb, Doc. Wollensky was real talkative. He told us the two of you had something you couldn't talk about—said Tony bragged he had this one thing over you. He thinks you offed Tony to keep whatever it was hush-hush.''

Trying to appear relaxed when his gut was suddenly tied in a knot—a too-familiar feeling he'd thought was in his past—Dermot said, "I wouldn't take Bingo Wollensky's word for anything, Detectives. He, like most of the residents of Heartland, has a problem with the truth.''

"Do *you?*'' Walker asked.

And Norelli followed up with, "Let's look at your situation, Mr. O'Rourke. We find your laptop under Tony's bed—''

"He *was* a thief.''

"—his roommate says you shared a secret, the guard on duty saw you in your office barely a half hour before the estimated time of death, a parishioner saw you at St. Peter's the night before—the same night the velvet rope used to hang Tony Vargas from the chandelier base disappeared from its stand near the confessional. Furthermore, not only was Tony your patient, but a decade ago, he was your altar boy. He must have known a lot about you, right?''

Dermot couldn't keep the irony from his tone. "Why don't you gentlemen spell it out for me."

"This business Wollensky brought up won't let me go," Norelli said. "I keep thinking, what if Tony knew something about 'Father Dermot' from the old days? Something that—if brought to light now—could ruin your very nice shrink career, if not put you in the slammer? What would you do to keep that secret...well...*secret?*"

"Did you kill Tony to keep him quiet?" Walker demanded to know.

"You're barking up the wrong tree, Detectives."

But they didn't look convinced.

Sweat trickled down Dermot's spine. He knew they were only doing their job. But he also knew he was innocent. And sometimes innocent people landed in jail. What a weird coincidence—his going to confession at his old church the night before, the same night the unique murder weapon had disappeared.

"Look, I can't tell you what you want to know. I didn't share any secret with Tony, but I was his confessor. Maybe that's what he was referring to. Anything you want to know about our sessions as therapist and patient—you've got it. I already told you that. But anything he admitted to in the confessional is off-limits."

Dermot feared he knew what the ex-con had been jawing about. As a priest, he had listened to Tony's confession years ago...had offered him absolution...but he'd never repeated what Tony had told him to a living soul, though he'd tried his best to make things right.

Unfortunately, the seal of the confessional didn't

end simply because a man realized the vocation he'd chosen was a mistake he couldn't go on making.

Even now Dermot was bound to silence.

WISHING SHE WERE A FLY on the wall inside the interrogation room, Detective Stella Jacobek paced the chipped, old ceramic-floored hallway outside. As an Area 3 detective, she had no business being here, even though she'd known Tony Vargas for most of his scummy life.

But how could she *not* be here when Dermot O'Rourke was in trouble?

She'd hardly been able to believe it. when she'd heard Dermot was being brought in for questioning for something they'd found on his laptop. She'd used her contacts to find out when he would be in the station. He might have been a hellion in his youth—how many times had she heard older parishioners say he'd been bad to the bone and were still shocked he'd become a priest?—and she might not have seen him for nearly a dozen years, but she owed him and meant to cover his back.

No matter how torn she was about seeing him again, she would put her doubts aside.

Even if Dermot had means, opportunity and a so-called motive—not to mention a violent past—Stella didn't believe he would kill anyone. Though he'd turned in his collar, he was an activist for social change and a therapist, and as such, continued to help people, even as he had helped her get through the darkest hours in her life. Now their roles were reversed and she could do no less for him.

Dermot O'Rourke was not a killer—on that, she would stake her life.

The interrogation room door snapped open and a voice drifted out to the hall. "You're free to go, Mr. O'Rourke. For now. In the meantime, don't leave the city."

And whether or not she was ready for him, Dermot was suddenly there. He didn't see her at first as he gathered himself together after what must have been an emotionally exhausting session, but she saw him, all six foot one of lean muscle encased in a tailored taupe suit, his dark reddish-brown hair punctuating a scowl that hardened his otherwise handsome face.

Her insides fluttered and she did her best to tamp down the old longing, with little success. Pushing a strand of golden-brown hair back into its loose knot at the nape of her neck, she wished she were wearing something other than her usual slacks and jacket with an open-necked blouse. Something more feminine. Attractive.

And then he saw her. Recognition instantly hit him, and he did a double take.

"Star Jacobek, is that really you?"

"Detective Stella Jacobek," she corrected him, though she didn't mind him calling her by the old nickname.

"I'm impressed."

He appeared impressed. His thick burnt-brown eyebrows arched over amazing green eyes. "It's good to see you, if not under these circumstances. Your boys made a mistake."

Just then, Norelli and Walker left the interrogation room. She knew them well enough to know they weren't going to like her getting cozy with their only suspect. Walker spotted her with Dermot and whacked his partner in the arm to look. Both detectives glared at her.

Ignoring them, she concentrated on Dermot. "Can we get outta here? We need to talk in private."

They agreed to meet at Brew Station, a café a few miles east, near the University of Illinois Chicago campus, a location on the way home for them both.

The ten-minute drive down the Eisenhower Expressway and through the expanding university area gave Stella some time to pull herself together, to remind herself she wasn't nineteen anymore. That's how old she'd been when Dermot had come to St. Peter's as a young priest and first heard her confession.

And that's how old she'd been when he'd literally saved her life.

Though he'd been from the neighborhood, he was older than she, so Stella hadn't known him before he'd come back as a newly ordained priest. She'd heard about his youthful reputation and his stints in juvy—older parishioners hadn't kept the gossip to themselves—but she'd never actually seen that side of him. Not at first. He'd been a little rough around the edges compared to the other priests she'd known, but he'd come through for her when she'd needed help.

Now she was a cop. A new detective. And this time Dermot needed *her* help rather than the other way around.

All she had to do was convince him of that.

It wasn't going to be easy. Not convincing him.

Not dealing with the renewed connection for her, either. She'd put the past behind her and just seeing Dermot stirred it all up again in her mind.

But she had to do it. Had to pay her debt.

Norelli had the reputation of being like a dog with a bone. He thought he smelled a murderer and he would do his best to get Dermot convicted unless they found another viable suspect.

"So what's going on with you, Star?" Dermot asked once they settled into the café. "How has life been treating you?"

She heard the concern in his voice. That aspect of him certainly hadn't changed. And *he* was the one with the problem.

"A lot better than in the old days," she told him. "Police work agrees with me."

"I can see that."

The way he looked at her made her flush.

But then he asked, "So what is this? A little undercover work? You getting me to confess?"

The heat in her face doubled. "You can't believe that, Dermot."

"Then what is it you want from me?"

"The truth."

"And that differs from getting a confession…how?"

"I want to hear it *from you* that you didn't murder Tony."

Dermot stared at her evenly and said, "I didn't have anything to do with his death."

"Okay." She'd told herself he couldn't have done it, but having him say it made the tightness she'd been feeling inside relax. Her gut instincts made her a good detective, and she was going to trust them now. She would swear he was telling her the truth. "Then I want to help you."

"Why?"

"Because I owe you."

"You owe me nothing."

Before she could argue, the waitress came and took their orders.

Then, before Dermot could try to dissuade her, she asked, "So what *did* Norelli find on your laptop?"

"Session notes with Tony. My observation that blackmail could get him killed. They suggested it was personal. And before you ask, it wasn't."

"I wasn't going to ask." If she'd thought it possible that Dermot could be guilty, she wouldn't be here. "Any idea of who Tony might have been blackmailing?"

"His associates were criminals."

Stella remembered Tony liked to dance around the truth. "What about this secret Wollensky said you had?"

"Wollensky was just mouthing off like Tony did to him. Trust me, there is no secret. You remember how Tony liked to puff up his importance."

"Yeah, right."

So why did she get the feeling there was more to it? That Dermot wasn't telling her everything?

Or maybe being this close to him simply unnerved her and she was imagining things. She whiteknuckled her coffee mug and prayed her weakness didn't show.

They sat in upholstered chairs before the unused fireplace—it was warm for late October and the air-conditioning was still on. A buzz surrounded them, voices of laughing and talking patrons, mostly students, but it was white noise to her, stuff she could let fall into the background, while she made her proposal clear.

"You don't really understand what Norelli and Walker are gonna do to you, Dermot. They'll probe every aspect of your life."

"I already feel probed."

"They've barely started. They're already talking to your friends, your neighbors, your relatives. They'll go through your finances to see if there've been any big additions or withdrawals lately. They'll be looking for anything to tie you in personally to the victim."

"But they won't find anything, because there's nothing to find."

"Even the implication of guilt will make headlines, and what do you think that'll do to your professional life?"

Stella had done her homework and knew Dermot worked for a national activist organization that helped people in low-income communities repair their lives and improve their communities. His work depended on grants, and grants depended on goodwill, and goodwill depended on reputation. If his went south, then so would his job.

"Before the people you work with realize you're innocent, your counseling program at the Humboldt Park Center for Change will be in shambles." She knew that particular program was his baby.

"Don't hold back, tell it like it is."

Stella started, then recognized the irony for what it was. An admission. She was preaching to the choir.

He already knew how this was going to go down. Of course he would. Though it might have been another life as far as he was concerned, Dermot had been through the system, something she was sure he could never forget.

"So what do you suggest?" he asked.

"Let me help you."

"And ruin everything you've worked so hard to get? I don't think so."

"I wouldn't even be a cop if not for you."

"You don't know that."

"I know it. You saved my life."

"I don't think he meant to kill you."

Stella swallowed hard. Even after all these years, the details of her attack were clear in her mind. Her rapist had been carrying. He might have used the weapon…after…if Dermot hadn't come to her rescue.

Closing her eyes, she remembered the expression of pity on Dermot's face while he'd gathered her clothes around her and helped her off the ground. Though she had known her rapist, she'd refused to press charges against Rick Lamey. He'd threatened that if she did, her younger sister would be next. But Dermot had assured her everything would be all right, had promised he would see to things personally.

Later, she'd heard Lamey had been found beaten and bloody in an alley the following night, and she'd known—priest or not—Dermot had done what she hadn't been able to do.

Had that been the moment she'd fallen in love with him? Or had it been when he'd convinced her she could find her way to taking power over what happened to her? She'd done that by applying to the Police Academy.

Soon after that, Dermot had removed his collar and disappeared from her life. She'd heard he was back some months before, volunteering with the ex-cons at Heartland House, though she hadn't seen him until now.

Stella opened her eyes and realized Dermot was staring at her. Was he remembering, as well? How could he not? How could he forget seeing her so vulnerable? Stella's throat tightened. If there was one thing she didn't want from him, it was pity. Any attraction she'd been feeling fizzled at the thought and left her nerve endings raw.

Not that it changed what she had to do.

"If not my life, you saved me in another way, then," she said. "You gave me direction. Purpose."

"You were a strong girl, Star. You would have found all that without me."

"Maybe, but we'll never know." She wanted to prove that she was strong *now*. That there was no room for pity in her life. "Let me help you."

"It'll cost you."

Perhaps with her job, she knew. If she turned her back on the law she served…but Dermot was innocent. And innocent men were sometimes convicted. No matter how difficult this was going to be for her, no matter the personal or professional cost to herself, Stella couldn't take the chance that he might go to jail for a crime he didn't commit.

"I know the chances. My decision. Let me do this for you." She thought he would continue to fight her, but his hesitation showed her a slight chink in his armor. "Dermot, please. I wouldn't be able to live with myself if I didn't help prove you're innocent."

"How?"

"I'm gonna call in a favor from some people I know. A really big favor."

HOPING HE WASN'T *MAKING* a big mistake, Dermot followed Stella toward the century-old building with a restored pale-green-tiled facade and a neon sign identifying it as Club Undercover. The entertainment destination was in the eclectic Bucktown-Wicker Park area on Chicago's north side. Along with restaurants and boutiques, bars and cafés, the club sat on Milwaukee Avenue, an angled street with a distant view of the downtown Chicago skyline.

The city had been blessed with a bout of Indian summer—unseasonably warm days and crisp but comfortable nights. Standing on the corner, a threadbare man hawked *Streetwise,* the newspaper of the homeless, to anyone who would come up with a buck. On an evening walk, a Mexican family strolled past them, the grandmother swaying to the music oozing from the club. Twenty-somethings with wild hair and tattoos and body piercings waited in line to get inside along with thirty-something professionals in designer wear.

And Stella walked right past them all, ignoring protests that she wait her turn.

Dermot followed, his discomfort at pushing through the crowd vying with his discomfort at putting his life into the hands of some secret organization she jokingly called Team Undercover. She'd told him that, a few months before, an old friend from the old neighborhood who worked here had played body-guard to a stalking victim. Blade Stone, bartender and former military man, and a few others had helped Stella keep the woman safe and nail her stalker.

What would make people who didn't know him want to help him, perhaps in defiance of the law? the therapist in Dermot wondered. What would make him trust them? He certainly didn't trust the system.

Stella. She made the difference.

He trusted *her*.

"Stay with me," she said, grabbing his hand and plunging down the staircase.

As Dermot followed her downstairs toward the lower-level entrance, he couldn't help but admire the view before him. The golden-brown hair demurely coiled at the nape of Stella's neck didn't minimize her attractiveness. Tonight she wore a print skirt, whose thin material fluttered around her long legs, and a soft gold sweater that revealed her neck and shoulders and accentuated her full breasts. Her body was buff due to her physical training, but in a wom-anly way that made Dermot's mouth go dry when he thought too closely on it.

He had to stop this. She was helping him as a friend. Friends were all they could ever be.

She glanced back at him, and her lips, softly blushed with a pink-gold luster, were curved in a smile. "Almost there!" she shouted over the music blasting out of the club.

Raising his voice, Dermot said, "I forgot how noisy it is to be young."

"I've simply forgotten how to be young," Stella admitted.

Undoubtedly it was difficult for her to remember she'd been young once, considering she'd lost her innocence in a dark alley a dozen years before.

The reminder clenched Dermot's gut.

Was she healed now? he wondered. Really healed deep inside? Or did she put on a good front during the day, while her sleep was still filled with nightmares?

Hopefully time had worked its magic on her. Not that she would ever forget.

Nor would he.

Stella pulled him right up to a woman at the door, whose black hair was striped with electric blue, saying, "We're here to see Blade."

The hostess stepped aside and waved them into a cave of glowing neon and music that vibrated the floor beneath his Italian leather loafers.

They skirted the red dance floor awash with gyrating couples and headed for the blue glow of the bar. There, a big man wielded a martini shaker like a weapon. How appropriate, Dermot thought wryly, considering what Stella had told him about Blade. If his long, dark hair pulled back from high cheekbones and a straight-bridged nose and tied with a leather thong were any indication, the man had claim to some Native American ancestry.

The bartender spotted them and grinned. "Hey, Star, good to see you. This your date?" he asked as they settled on stools before him.

Stella neatly avoided the question, merely saying, "Blade Stone, meet Dermot O'Rourke."

"O'Rourke," Blade echoed. "As in the priest?"

"Ex-priest," Dermot said, shaking the other man's

hand and wondering how much Stella had told her friend about him.

Blade's dark stare got to him. The big man was taking his measure…as if judging him…not that he could possibly know all about the past…

"I heard about you growing up. And now I finally get to meet the man who saved my best friend's life," Blade said. "I'll always regret I was in the military when she was targeted. But you were there for her. Thank you." Then he turned his attention back to Stella. "What can I get you?"

"A few minutes with your boss. We, um, need all of your help."

Stella had told him about Gideon, owner of the club and a man with an enigmatic past; Logan, security chief and ex-CPD detective; Cassandra, hostess and former magician's assistant; Gabe, another man of mystery.

Blade's gaze drilled into him. Apparently understanding Stella's vague request, he nodded.

Dermot felt as if he'd earned the ex-military man's seal of approval and wondered if he would have to pass a similar inspection with all members of Team Undercover.

Chapter Two

Gideon was dealing with the books—his least favorite task as owner of Club Undercover—when a knock at the door got his attention.

"Come in," he said, glad for the interruption.

He closed the ledger and slid it to a corner of his black-lacquered desk as Blade Stone walked in followed by his childhood friend Detective Stella Jacobek and a man Gideon had never seen before.

"Blade, Stella." He glanced at the stranger.

"Dermot O'Rourke," the man announced himself.

"I need a favor," Stella said.

Gideon could tell she wasn't happy having to ask. "Maybe we should get the others in here."

As Blade said, "Already done," John Logan and then Gabe Conner strolled through the door.

"Cass'll be here in a minute," Logan said, flicking some invisible speck off his impeccable suit lapel.

Gideon made the introductions, ending with "Gabe is taking over as my security chief. Logan finally agreed to take back his detective shield."

"You're on the force again?" Stella asked.

"Monday morning."

"Good. What area?"

"Four. Violent Crimes."

"Even better," Stella said. "We may need your help there."

"Help where?" Cassandra asked as she breezed into the room on four-inch heels, which made her a formidable figure in her teal velvet dress and hair so red it appeared to be on fire. "Do we have a new case?"

"Meet a friend of Stella's," Blade said, indicating Dermot.

As Cass shook his hand her smile faded, and she grew immediately silent. Which put up Gideon's antennae. But he turned to Stella and Dermot. "Why don't you sit and tell me what you need from us," he suggested.

Cass backed up against the indigo wall and stared at Dermot O'Rourke, while the duo took the black leather chairs on the other side of his desk.

Gideon watched him, too, as Stella told his story in shorthand. Dermot seemed a little uncomfortable as Stella went over the details that pointed to him as the only suspect.

Psychotherapist volunteers time at halfway house… ex-con found dead…supposed secret between the two…cryptic message on laptop…not enough to make arrest…

Not yet.

If Dermot was guilty, he didn't show it, Gideon thought. Blade appeared convinced of the man's innocence, no doubt because he trusted Stella's judgment. Logan and Gabe both seemed to be neutral as they listened. But Cass's sharp gaze on the potential client didn't let up.

"If you help me with Dermot," Stella said, "I will do what I can to help you with other clients in the future."

"I'm for it," Blade said.

No objections from Logan and Gabe. And while Cass didn't voice any objections, neither did her normally bubbly nature surface.

"I think we need to discuss the matter in private," Gideon told Stella.

"Of course." Her expression worried, Stella rose immediately and tugged at her companion's sleeve. "We'll wait at the bar."

"Thanks for listening, anyway," Dermot said. "Whatever you decide."

Dermot followed Stella out of the room.

The door had barely closed behind them before Blade asked, "What's the problem, Gideon?"

"Ask Cass."

Her eyes went wide. "I don't have a problem."

"That's why you're so chatty."

"I don't have to talk all the time," she protested, at which Logan barked a laugh. Reddening, she glared at the soon-to-be-ex-security chief. "I don't!"

"What is it that has you spooked about Dermot O'Rourke?" Gideon pressed.

She shrugged and brushed it off with a breezy, "Nothing."

So Cass wasn't going to spill whatever was bothering her, which deepened Gideon's curiosity.

Although she would never readily talk about it, Cassandra Freed was psychic and they all knew it.

Now Blade and Logan and Gabe were staring at her with questioning expressions. She flicked at a red curl with a long teal fingernail and tried to appear unfazed.

But Gideon knew when she was picking up signals. Though he didn't like the fact that Cass wouldn't talk, he was certain it wasn't that the man was guilty. So she must be picking up on something else.

"So you think we should take the case?" Gideon asked her directly.

Her gaze shifted away from him as she said, "Yes, of course. Stella has kept the details of what we do for people to herself, and if she thinks this guy is worth the trouble, then he must be."

"What about you two?" he asked Logan and Gabe.

"Come Monday I'll certainly be in a position to help," Logan said. "I say go for it."

"I'm the newcomer to this group," Gabe said. "I'll go along with whatever you decide."

"And you know where I stand," Blade said.

Gideon nodded. "All right, then. We'll do it. Blade, you ask around Pilsen, see what people remember about Father Dermot and what they think of him now that he's volunteering with ex-cons. Gabe, you do a full computer search on the man's history…and on the victim's. Logan, when you get into the Area 4 office—"

"Got it."

Even if he wasn't assigned to it, Logan would familiarize himself with the case, Gideon knew. He would be their eyes and ears in the CPD as long as he stayed low profile. Once the detectives on the case knew where Stella Jacobek stood, they wouldn't have any use for her.

"What about me?" Cass asked.

"I thought you might want to stay out of this one."

"No way! We're a team, aren't we?"

Yeah, Team Undercover, a group of outcasts helping the desperate when they had nowhere else to turn.

No cover charged…no ID required…secrecy guaranteed.

"Start by acting as a support system," he told her. "This case seems important to Stella. Personal. Maybe she needs a friend."

Though Cass gave him an I-know-what-you're-doing look, she didn't argue.

Helping others had given him his life purpose.

And he knew that Cass, having spent the better part of two years in jail for a crime she didn't commit, wouldn't want to see another innocent incarcerated.

That was assuming Dermot O'Rourke was innocent, not only of murder but whatever was hidden in his past.

"ARE YOU SURE you don't have any idea who Tony Vargas was blackmailing?" Stella asked Dermot when he let her into his office the next morning.

While the decorating budget obviously had been modest, and some of the furniture undoubtedly secondhand, the room would put a patient at ease. The pale-blue walls were calming—big windows lined the wall on the north, giving plenty of light; no therapist couch. Two fancy chairs seemed to be the only touch of luxury, and she suspected Dermot had paid for them out of his own pocket.

"I don't have a clue as to Tony's target," Dermot told her. "Sit."

Stella wasn't ready to get cozy. While Dermot made himself comfortable, she paced, taking in the framed posters breaking up the long wall opposite the windows.

"Dermot, I know denying knowledge of the black-mail target is your official story—"

"It's the truth."

"Therapist-patient privilege is at the discretion of the patient, and considering Tony's dead, he certainly can't object." Stella wanted to believe him, but she had to make sure they were clear. "Besides which, whatever he told you involves a past crime. Or a future one. It isn't the same as the seal of the confessional."

At which Dermot bristled. "I'm aware of all that, and I still don't know. Tony liked to talk, whether to get something off his conscience or to brag, but he was always careful how much he said."

"What did he say exactly?" she asked, taking the vacant chair, which immediately rocked backward.

"We were discussing Tony's plans for the future. I asked if he had anything in mind that would be productive, as in going to school to get some kind of training so he could find a decent job. He told me once he made his big score, he wouldn't need to work for a while."

"And from that you got blackmail?"

"From that I informed him it wouldn't be in his best interest to tell me about any crimes he intended to commit, that if he told me about a crime, I was obligated to report it."

"No patient-therapist privilege there," she agreed.

"Tony said he wasn't planning on committing any

crime, just accepting a cut of the wealth. The definition of *accessory* escaped him, I suppose. Not that I had any details. But I did ask who was going to be generous enough to share the spoils, and all Tony said was, someone who wouldn't want him to mess things up.''

''So he was blackmailing another criminal.''

''That's my conclusion.''

''And you told Norelli and Walker all this.''

Dermot laughed. ''Not that they believed me. Not without a name.''

''And you're sure you don't have one.''

''You don't believe me, either?''

Her chair was so comfortable she could see why clients relaxed. But being this close to Dermot, in such a vulnerable position, she couldn't unwind.

''Of course I believe you, Dermot. But in your sessions, Tony must have talked about associates.''

''Yeah, like Mack the Knife, the leader of his cell block, and Bugger Bob.''

''But he didn't mention anyone from the old neighborhood?''

''Other than Johnny Rincon…I'd have to look at my notes.''

''Johnny Rincon.'' Stella's gut tightened. ''The one offender from the old days who I targeted but was never able to put behind bars.''

Johnny had been trouble from day one in high school. She and Blade had stuck together to keep out of his gang. Eventually Blade had fought Johnny, had left him with a scarred face, a permanent reminder that Blade was no one to mess with. Johnny was guilty of so many things, but she'd never been able to get the proof she needed to put him where he belonged. And her detective's shield had taken her out of Pilsen, so she guessed she never would.

Unless…

"What about Johnny?" she asked.

"Tony blamed Johnny for letting him take the rap on the theft that put him behind bars."

Stella's instincts perked up. "Anything more on that?"

"Nothing I remember specifically. Again I'll have to check my notes. One or two sessions a week for more than three months is a lot of talking."

Stella nodded. "If I were you, I'd go over your records with a fine-tooth comb before Norelli subpoenas them."

"He doesn't have to subpoena them. All he has to do is ask. I've already made a copy."

"Good. Then see if there's anyone else Tony sounded obsessed over."

"If it's there, I'll be on it."

Dermot's gaze was steady on her, making Stella self-conscious. He was counting on her. She couldn't fail him, not with what she owed him.

"Now, what about you?" she asked, her voice tight. She wanted to know everything about him, wanted to savor every personal detail. But she kept it professional. "Did you get yourself a lawyer?"

"I don't trust lawyers."

"But you need one. You've gotta protect yourself. Maybe you've never had a good one. I'll ask Lynn Cross who she recommends."

"The lawyer Blade brought to Undercover?"

Stella nodded. "Blade's fiancée now. Lynn's specialty is divorce, but I'm sure she could recommend a good criminal lawyer.''

''Criminal,'' he echoed, then smiled at her. ''Great. But then, I always knew that about you.''

Warmth flushed through Stella at the compliment, and she squirmed at the reminder of their former relationship, of the fact that he knew what had happened to her.

So he thought she was great? Why? Because she'd put the attack behind her and made a life? Better than being pitied, she supposed.

Stella told herself to calm down and not try to dissect the compliment. Dermot wasn't like the guys who would feed a girl a load of bull to get what they wanted. He was up-front...unless it involved privileged information.

''One more thing,'' she said. ''Two velvet ropes disappeared from St. Peter's. Only one turned up around Tony's neck.''

''If you're suggesting I might have the other one, I can assure you I don't.''

''Good.'' Rocking the chair forward, she got to her feet. ''I should scram, give you some room. You probably have a client scheduled in soon, anyway.''

''I've put all my appointments on hold. I have some paperwork to take care of and then I'm done here until things are resolved.''

''But won't that hurt your program?''

''I have someone covering for me. My name in the papers would hurt the center more. We're waiting to hear on a big grant for the drug rehab program. I'm afraid any notoriety will blow it for the center, and we really need that money.''

"Then we'll have to make sure your name doesn't get in the papers other than in a positive way."

His voice lowered when he said, "From your lips…"

The way he was staring at her lips made Stella think he had something else in mind. Flushing, she told herself not to be foolish. The attraction had always been one way. And if there was something going on here, she couldn't act on it. The important thing was clearing Dermot's name. She had to stay focused.

She said, "If we all work together, we'll make sure you don't get convicted of a crime you didn't commit. I'm, uh, gonna take some comp time myself."

She knew Dermot wouldn't be content to sit around and twiddle his thumbs, and she couldn't let him run his own investigation.

"I can't ask you to do that, Star."

"You didn't. I'd be too distracted thinking of you. Of the trouble you're in," she amended. "You check over those records, and I'll see if I can get anything through the grapevine. Unfortunately, Logan won't be back at Area 4 until Monday." A lot could happen in two days, bad or good. "I can meet you back here and we can compare notes before going over to Club Undercover."

"Why don't I pick you up instead?"

"Yeah, sure."

Stella took out her pad and scribbled her address and phone number on a blank page. When she handed it to Dermot, his fingers brushed hers, and it was all she could do to act unaffected. Beneath her casual stance, her chest squeezed tight and her knees suddenly felt like rubber, and the idea of being alone with Dermot at her place was a little too cozy for her comfort.

Suddenly Stella suspected that clearing Dermot's name was going to be easier than working with him to get it done.

WORD HAD ALREADY SPREAD from the cop shop through the neighborhood: Stella was once again sticking her nose where it didn't belong.

Messing up carefully laid plans seemed to be her life's work.

Tony Vargas's murder had turned into a twofold master stroke. What a piece of cake that had been. Tony'd gotten onto the rickety chair as instructed. He'd even put the velvet rope around his own neck, attached it to the hook in the chandelier base himself. He'd pleaded through the whole thing, of course, weeping for mercy like a girl. But always weak, Tony had done what he was told, no doubt trusting he would get some last-minute reprieve.

When the chair had been kicked out from under him, the little weasel's expression of disbelief had been priceless.

Getting rid of a blackmailer had been the prime objective. But if Tony dead was the cake, then Dermot O'Rourke behind bars would be the icing.

And now it might never happen.

Despite all the careful planning to make it look like O'Rourke could be involved, he had an ally in the CPD determined to get him off. Detective Stella Jacobek.

Time to teach her another lesson.

Chapter Three

"Hey, Jacobek, what the hell is this I hear about you going against your own for a murderer?"

Sergeant Mack Johnson loomed over Stella's desk as she hung up the phone after talking to Lynn Cross, who'd readily agreed to put Dermot in touch with a top trial lawyer. Johnson was intimidating by his very size, yet normally good-natured. So, one look at the glowering expression on her superior's dark face ruined Stella's good mood.

"You know better than that, Mack. He's an *alleged* murderer," Stella countered, her throat tight. "But I swear to you Dermot didn't murder anyone—I'd bet my badge he's innocent."

"It just might *be* your badge, Jacobek."

She said, "Dermot is a personal friend," as if that would make him back off.

"Norelli and Walker are already making a stink. The lieutenant's breathing down my neck on this one." The man wiped a little sweat from where it trickled down his bald head. "Friend or not, stay out of the Vargas case."

"I can't do that, Mack." She winced when his face

grew even darker in response. He really wasn't going to like what she had to tell him next...unless she could finesse him into thinking it might get him off the hook. "But what I *can* do is remove myself from the lieutenant's eye for a few days. That way, I'm not officially working against anyone."

"You're going to make this into a public relations nightmare for the department!"

"I'll do my best not to," Stella promised. "I'll be discreet. But I can't sit back while a friend's life is being ruined—when he could spend time in prison for something he didn't do. I know you're a man of integrity, Sergeant, and you wouldn't let that happen to someone you cared about, either." Though he was still steaming, he didn't contradict her, so she casually added, "You know I have plenty of time due."

Detectives worked a ton of overtime. They didn't just start investigating a murder case and then take off when their shift was done. There were times when she'd worked three or four days straight without ever going home. And it was her option to take overtime pay or comp time.

Still, her chest tightened as she waited for a decision—it was Johnson's option to deny her time due if he so chose, and he might for her own good.

She figured Johnson was grappling with the separation of official sanction and her own personal need. He was angry with her, and part of her didn't blame him. She was going against her own.

"Mack, you know what kind of detective I am. I don't rest at night if I don't find the right answers. If I did, I might not have broken the Moore case."

She brought it up because he'd been particularly

eager to get that murder solved. One of the suspects had been an acquaintance of his, and her tireless work had cleared the guy. When his expression shifted, Stella knew she'd hit the right nerve.

"All right. Take a few days, then. Do what you have to do but keep a low profile."

"That's the idea," she agreed, relief allowing her to breathe normally again. "Thank you."

"And make sure you get your old cases out of the way first." With a curt nod, he strode away.

Stella felt curious eyes. Another detective and a couple of uniforms around the room were focused on her. No doubt having heard at least part of the exchange, they were waiting for her to say something.

Nodding at them instead, she got back to work, sorting through her caseload and picking the oldest cases that needed some kind of finding before she left.

Even knowing she would be free to do what she needed in a few hours, she was champing at the bit to get started. Obviously, she couldn't call Norelli or Walker for an update. From their expressions when they'd seen her with Dermot the afternoon before, she'd known they would view her involvement as a professional insult. At least come Monday, Logan would have the inside track at Area 4.

That gave her tonight and all of tomorrow to work on her own.

True to her word, she would keep a low profile if she could. She didn't want to lose the job that had become everything to her. But if it became a choice between the job and Dermot O'Rourke's life...

Stella simply hoped it would never come to that, because in her mind and heart, Dermot would always come first.

STELLA HADN'T STRAYED far from the old haunts, Dermot thought, only as far as Bridgeport, famous for being the south-side area of Chicago that had spawned more mayors than any other. The buildings were neat brick bungalows between rows of two and three flats. The streets were neat, too, as if daring any refuse to stray there. But autumn brought a new challenge of russet and gold raining down on them. Residents raked the leaves up as fast as they fell. An old guy was out there now, in the dark, doing his best to keep up with the dropping foliage.

Bridgeport—blue-collar but still more affluent than Pilsen, the neighborhood his gang had preyed on when they'd been looking for a quick score. Dermot had actually believed he'd been done with his past life and this part of the city, and here he was being dragged back to it all.

Maybe it was true, he thought, that you never outgrew your past.

He pulled up to the curb in front of a red-brick two-flat, whose bay windows were inset with stained glass trim, but before he could cut the engine, Stella was on the porch, waving at him to stay in the car. He watched her bound down the steps, her long-sleeved orange midriff sweater glowing under the streetlights and giving him a glimpse of flesh that made his mouth go dry. Her hair was loose, waving around her shoulders tonight, and as she approached the car, he imagined tangling his fingers in the long, luscious strands….

Then the car door opened, ending the fantasy.

"A man who's on time," Stella said, sliding into the passenger seat. "I like that."

"I thought you wanted a powwow before going to the club."

"You can talk while you drive, right?"

Her tone was light, but Dermot heard something in it that put him on notice. What? Was she afraid someone would see them together?

That thought eating at him, he said, "Seat belt," and pulled the car away from the curb.

Buckling up, she asked, "Did you get a chance to go over your notes on your sessions with Tony?"

Despite his slippery circumstances, Dermot found that he didn't want to talk about Tony or about himself. He wanted to talk about her, to find out what her life was like away from the world of violence that she had embraced. He wanted to know if she was okay. If she was happy. If she'd ever been in love. Not that it was any of his business.

Besides, that would be a dangerous path to follow. He could never be more to Stella than a friend unless she knew everything about him.

So, instead of interrogating her, he said, "I've gone over maybe half of Tony's session notes. So far, other than his jail mates and Johnny, the only person he talked about at length was Marta Ortiz."

"The alderman?"

"Who happens to have been his cousin. Heartland is her baby. She believes in rehabilitation and second chances, and believes the way to do it is with structure and reeducation. She had influence in the parole process and she made sure Tony was assigned to the halfway house for six months as a condition of his release.''

''I take it that didn't make him happy.''

Dermot turned south on Halsted Street, planning on taking it straight through Pilsen to the north side.

''I wouldn't say Tony was overjoyed. He figured Marta wanted to control him.''

''As in?''

''Making him see me, for one. Though, knowing Tony, he would have done so, anyway. He liked to get things off his chest.'' Dermot's mood darkened as he remembered the things Tony had confessed to all those years before. A confession that had changed Dermot's life. ''Even more, Tony liked the idea of talking to someone who couldn't repeat what he heard.''

The seal of the confessional….

''What else did he say about the alderman?''

''That she could be a raving lunatic when she was angry.''

''So he was afraid of his own cousin?''

''Let's say he was committed to not making her angry.''

''So, we have Johnny Rincon and Alderman Marta Ortiz—worlds apart. My bet's on Johnny, though.''

''Seems likely.''

''And if it is, I'll finally get to put him where he belongs.''

Would that mean she would finally put her past to rest? Dermot could only hope so.

''I'll go through the rest of my notes later tonight or tomorrow,'' he said, ''and see if I can short-list anyone else. By the way, kudos to Lynn Cross. She contacted Avery Stark who called me this afternoon. We worked a deal, so I'm covered if Norelli and Walker get serious about cuffing me.''

"Good, because as far as I know, you're still the only suspect. You very well may need someone to run legal interference while I work on this case.''

"*We*," he corrected her. "While *we* work on the case.''

She didn't say anything.

They quickly passed the edge of Chinatown, then Little Italy. It wasn't until they hit Greektown and were stuck in the stop-and-go of Saturday-night traffic that Stella suddenly asked, "What made you decide to become a priest, anyway? You shocked a whole lot of people.''

"Myself included," he admitted. "If you really want to know, I was headed down a wrong road. My dad disappeared on us, and there was Mom trying to take care of my brothers and me while working two jobs. Left a lot of time for a kid to get into trouble.''

"Or into a gang.''

"Yeah, I was an Eagle. Mom ragged on me about it all the time, but the more she harped, the more I was determined to do what I wanted. She swore I was killing her.''

"I'm sure you upset her, but isn't that a little overdramatic?''

"That was Mom, a real Irish drama queen. Irish as in from Ireland. When I was sixteen, I ended up in a juvenile home," he admitted, knowing his records were sealed. Unless Stella had gotten information about his past from a personal contact, she wouldn't know about this. "A kid was in a coma and the blame fell on me."

"Was it your fault?"

She was trying not to sound shocked, he realized, gripping the steering wheel tighter.

"I didn't start the fight. You know gang wars can be vicious. And I swear when we left the area, the guy was all right—bleeding but conscious. But obviously he was hurt worse than anyone figured. All I know is I was arrested and told that if he died, life as I knew it was over. Thank God he came out of it within the week."

"So fear got you on the straight-and-narrow."

"Fear and Father Padilla. He battered at me until I fought my way out of the gang, taught me that education was my ticket to a better life. I didn't even know how much I could learn until he started pushing me."

"You have a lot to thank him for, then."

"That I do. So I graduated, went to community college, got a scholarship to finish in Urbana. And then Mom got sick. A bad heart that got worse because of a major heart attack after a fight we had. The doctors predicted she could go anytime without a new heart, and she didn't believe in anything as unnatural as having someone else's heart put in her body...if she could have gotten one. Anyway, in Ireland, the youngest son was expected to go into the church. She told me that she wanted to see me ordained before she died."

"You went into a vocation because she wanted it for you? That wasn't fair."

"Her dying at fifty-one wasn't fair, either. When I

realized how sick she really was, the guilt got to me. She always said I'd be the death of her, and it looked like I would be. I talked to Father Padilla about the priest thing, and he encouraged me to consider whether or not I might have a vocation. I knew he wanted me to say yes.''

"He pressured you."

"No, not exactly. He wasn't like that. He talked about the advantages, though. Father Padilla was the one who turned my life around, and Mom was losing hers because of me.''

Dermot now knew he'd acted out of love and grief for what was coming, and out of guilt that he'd been part of it. He'd never given himself the chance to think his decision through properly, to realize that not having a vocation made a travesty of being ordained.

"I felt my studying at the seminary was the only thing that was keeping Mom alive—she barely saw me ordained before she died. Afterward I figured it was too late. I convinced myself I'd done the right thing.''

"But it wasn't."

He shook his head. "Not for me. I chafed under church politics every single day…'' *The seal of the confessional.* "…and I realized I wanted a family of my own. Then one day…I'd just had it.''

He'd already been considering leaving before Stella's attack. When he'd gone after Rick Lamey on his own—he'd wanted to kill the bastard and almost had—he'd known he crossed the line as a priest.

Another thing he'd never told her.

"You wanted a family," she said. "So why didn't you marry?"

"Actually, I did." Dermot turned the car up Milwaukee Avenue, wishing they were at the club already. "That didn't turn out so well, either."

"Your wife didn't die?" Stella asked, sounding horrified.

Dermot laughed. "Hardly. Laurie left me for another man. Not that she had one at the time. She simply chose to be free to find one who could give her the lifestyle she so desperately felt she deserved. We met when she was a college senior and I was picking up some advanced social work and psychology classes. I was blinded by her beauty and she was blinded by visions of the money she thought I would be making as therapist to the rich and famous."

"Um, you haven't done so badly for yourself."

"I'm comfortable," he admitted. "Comfortable wasn't good enough for her. She said that if I insisted on giving away my services—meaning the halfway house or wherever else I might have donated my time—we would never be able to afford the home or other things she expected."

"Ouch. She wasn't good enough for you, Dermot."

Not wanting to open that vein any further, Dermot was relieved to see the glowing neon of the Club Undercover sign ahead.

He'd done his best to make the marriage work, despite the fact that Laurie had been his second choice when Stella would have been his first.

Not that it would ever have happened.

In helping Stella through the aftermath of the rape, he'd developed romantic feelings for her. Falling in love with a woman had given him another jolt of reality, an additional reason to leave the priesthood. But fearing that Stella might always associate him with that horrible aspect of her past, knowing he could never be completely honest with her, he never told her how he'd felt.

Instead, he'd simply left her to her own life, knowing the seal of the confessional would always stand between them.

AS THEY ENTERED Club Undercover and headed for Gideon's office, Stella couldn't help but think about Dermot's reason for taking on a career not of his own choosing. How could she wish he'd done otherwise? If not for his having been a priest, she wouldn't be a cop.

Hell, she might not be alive.

Perhaps Dermot found contentment in his work…but as Stella well knew, work wasn't everything. She only wished such a good and honest man could find the personal happiness that eluded him.

With her, an idiot of a voice whispered in her head, when she knew that was never going to happen.

Once in Gideon's office, they quickly brought the team up to speed about her taking days off and Dermot's getting a lawyer—though that word had already been passed along through Blade via Lynn—and about Tony's adversarial relationships with Johnny Rincon and Marta Ortiz.

"Johnny Rincon again," Gideon said with a glower.

And Blade muttered, "Seems like good ol' Johnny'll haunt us forever."

Remembering Blade had another run-in with their

old nemesis while protecting Lynn, Stella said, "If Johnny is guilty of murder, I'll do whatever is necessary to prove it and get him off the streets."

"You know better than to mess with him," Blade warned her.

"It's my job."

"You're not on the job—"

Dermot interrupted, saying, "Stella's with me now. I won't let anything happen to her."

Stella caught her breath. With *him?* An odd thing to say. But his expression was so determined, his gaze on her so piercing, she was caught. She remembered Rick Lamey. And the kid Dermot had put in a coma. In that instant she felt his power.

Then she realized the room had gone silent. The others stared at Dermot with interest and some surprise. Everyone but Cassandra, who wore an odd expression. Cass knew things…*about Dermot?*

"So where do you plan on starting?" Gideon asked. "Ahem, Stella?"

Realizing the attention had shifted to her, Stella snapped back and took a deep breath. "Pilsen, of course. My father's cousin Frank still lives there. He owns a car repair shop and parts store and has the pulse of the neighborhood, so to speak. I'm going to see what the word on the street might be."

Wondering if Blade would insist on escorting her, she glanced his way. His features were set in neutral, though his arms were crossed in front of him as if he was holding himself back. Which he very well might be. But Dermot had made it clear that he would take care of her, and her old friend was respecting that commitment.

After they broke up a few minutes later, and the others got to work for the night and she headed for the ladies' lounge, Stella was still thinking about Dermot's unexpected avowal. He'd sounded so protective, exactly as he had the night he'd saved her.

Though a thrill shot through her at the realization, she wasn't certain if he was simply backing her as a partner in this investigation...or if there was some more personal reason to it.

The still-empty ladies' lounge was luxurious, decorated in the jewel tones of the club. Sapphire carpeting...emerald upholstered chairs...topaz walls... even the blobs of colored glass framing the large makeup mirror were gem colored.

After freshening up, Stella sat on a ruby-upholstered stool before that mirror and pulled comb and lipstick out of her pocket. She never carried a purse—too damn inconvenient—unless she was at some formal function, and there weren't many of those in her life. She was smudging her lips with a golden orange gloss when Cass entered and threw herself down in the next stool. But rather than primping, Cass used the mirror to connect with Stella.

"So how are you holding up?"

"I'm doing fine. Why wouldn't I be?"

"You just put yourself in a difficult position with the police department. High stress."

Stella ran the comb through her loose hair. "My job *is* stress. I can take more."

"I'm sure you can. But if you ever need to talk…"

"Sure. Thanks." Wondering why Cass really had joined her, Stella eyed her via the mirror. "What is it with you and Dermot? You don't like him. Why?"

Cass squirmed a bit. "I don't *dislike* him."

"But you change around him. Your smile disappears and you get too serious. You did last night and again just now. There's got to be a reason."

"Nothing, really. Just…a feeling."

"What kind of feeling?"

"Like Dermot goes to some dark place inside himself. Like he's torturing himself about something."

Wondering if Cass had picked up on the vibes due to their conversation about the kid Dermot had put in a coma, she said, "All of us do that once in a while."

"You're right," Cass said. "I just caught him at a bad time."

Cass was avoiding telling her more, Stella thought. She'd interviewed enough offenders to know.

"Exactly how psychic are you?" Stella asked.

"I never said—"

"You didn't have to. Blade did."

Cass made a face. Rolled her eyes. Stella waited her out. She was good at waiting. It was how she got offenders to spill. Cass was far easier than the scum she dealt with. It only took a minute for her to cave.

"Look, I don't usually get pictures. No movie runs through my head. I just…sense emotions…sometimes know things. I can't explain."

Can't or won't? Stella wondered.

"But you don't know anything about Dermot other than sensing some kind of darkness."

Cass hesitated, then said, "I see you there with him," making Stella's pulse jump. "But that's all. I swear."

Her and Dermot together. In danger? She assumed the darkness meant danger.

"Have you tried looking deeper?"

"It's not something to fool with."

"I don't want to fool with it," Stella said. "I want to nail a murderer."

"And you will." Cass rose. "I need to get to work. The hordes are arriving."

With that, she nearly ran from the room.

Leaving Stella wondering how dark was dark. Was Cass sensing the past?

Or was it a warning for the future?

Chapter Four

Anxious to get her private investigation started for real, Stella stood on the sidewalk in front of St. Adalbert Church as Sunday mass let out. In the midst of a poverty-stricken, gang-infested neighborhood that only in recent years had seen the beginnings of gentrification, the century-old church remained an opulent icon, testimony to the strong faith and generosity of its mostly have-not parishioners.

Strangers to Stella filed down the church steps this morning, though she did recognize a few of the older, Polish-speaking people. Then she spotted the person she'd come here to find—her dad's cousin who never missed the Polish-language service.

"Hey, Frank!" she yelled, waving him over.

In the middle of a conversation with a young kid with gangbanger written all over him—from his combat boots to his leather stadium jacket, from the green bandanna around his forehead to cropped hair shaved with a lightning-bolt design—Frank Jacobek signaled her to wait a moment. If the downward curve of his mouth and his thick eyebrows furrowing together were any indication, he was angry.

Stella couldn't help wondering why Frank might be giving a gang member a piece of his mind. He wasn't as young as he used to be, and she couldn't help worrying that he might be sticking his nose into trouble he didn't need.

That was Frank Jacobek, though—old-school and as tough as they came.

Finished with his conversation, Frank turned his back on the kid, who glared after him before stomping off. Connecting with her, Frank's expression lightened and his lips turned up in a smile.

Swooping down the steps, he gave her a big bear hug and sloppily smooched her cheek. "You haven't been by to see me in months. Where you been keeping yourself, Star?"

Frank had been the one to give her the nickname after explaining that Stella *meant* star.

"Working. I got promoted, remember." She ignored the guilt that surfaced at the reminder of her neglect.

"And here I thought maybe you finally had yourself a serious boyfriend."

"Not yet."

Stella blinked away the instant vision of Dermot's handsome features and sexy smile from her mind's eye. She *wished*. The heat of embarrassment—or was it desire flashing through her?—made her cross her arms protectively in front of her.

She couldn't believe Frank was still asking about boyfriends as if she were a kid.

"I don't know about young men these days, passing up a smart, beautiful girl like you."

"Maybe they're afraid if they get out of line, I'll arrest 'em."

They laughed together as they used to, as if they hadn't seen less and less of each other over the years, and Stella regretted she hadn't found time for Frank. After all, they were family and both alone—his third wife having left him a few years before. He couldn't stay married and he'd never had kids, maybe the reason he'd taken such interest in her and her sister, Anna. Frank was the only family Stella had left in the city. Her widowed mom had remarried and moved to the suburbs, and her sister's job had taken her out of state.

"So what's up, Star?"

"Can we go someplace private to talk? It's important."

Frank's expression grew serious once more. "You still like pancakes with pecans and peaches?"

"Haven't outgrown them yet," she admitted.

"Then we go to my place where I'll make 'em for you."

Stella couldn't resist. "What are we waiting for?"

Frank had walked to church, so Stella drove.

Though in his late fifties now, his brown hair threaded with gray, his face sagging a little more than it used to, Frank Jacobek was still a powerful-looking man with impressive shoulders that stretched the made-to-order gray suit. He was looking good. As a kid, she'd simply thought of him as being big enough to fill a doorway, but maybe that's because he'd intimidated her.

After her dad had died when she was a kid, his cousin Frank had been the self-proclaimed patriarch of the family, helping her mom financially when needed and becoming sort of a father figure to Stella and her sister. He'd even taken them all on summer vacations to his cabin in Wisconsin, where he'd given them a taste of living with nature. Great times. On the other hand, true to his appearance, he'd been a strict disciplinarian, a trait she hadn't much appreciated as a kid. But with some years on her, Stella had no doubt Frank had helped mold her into the strong, ethical person she was today.

Only a few blocks from the church, Frank's place sat over his car-parts store and flanked the repair shop. Being Sunday, both businesses were closed.

They entered the frame two-story from the side entrance and climbed to the second floor. The old wood stairs creaked and groaned every bit as much as they had twenty years ago. A fanciful kid, she used to think they would collapse on her one day. Even now she wasn't so sure they wouldn't.

"Home, sweet home," Frank said, his gravelly voice sounding happy about being there. "Take a load off. Put on a CD. I have a home stereo system, you know. And cable. All the premium channels."

But Stella followed him down the hall, pausing to look at the framed photographs lining the long wall. There was one of her and her mom and Anna in front of Frank's cabin. Other pictures of Wisconsin brought back old memories, including one of a large house on a bluff overlooking Lake Geneva—the one they'd all picked out together as their favorite.

Smiling at the memories, Stella sauntered into the kitchen, saying, "I don't need to be entertained, not when I can watch you cook."

"Suit yourself."

Stella equated what Frank had done with the ancient apartment to his driving those old Beamers or Jags he salvaged and repaired. Some years back, the entire living space had been renovated in a modest manner, except for the kitchen, which he'd expanded by knocking out some walls. Only the best would do for a man who loved to cook as much as he loved to eat. His granite counters, island workspace and top-of-the-line appliances would do any chef proud.

"I'll make coffee," she volunteered as he removed his suit jacket and hung it on a wall peg.

"All right. Then you'll sit." He swung open the refrigerator door and pulled a carton of eggs from the interior. "Bacon or chicken sausage?"

"Bacon, please."

Within minutes, the aroma of fresh French roast coffee mixed with frying bacon filled the kitchen. Stella perched on a stool and watched Frank finish mixing the pancake batter.

"So what's up, Star?" he asked again.

Stella wanted to say she'd simply missed him and had decided to correct the situation, but she couldn't lie. "I need information, and I thought I would come to the man who has his fingers on the pulse of the neighborhood."

That car repair shop of his was as busy and filled with as much gossip as any hair salon.

"I'm not in the loop like I used to be." He ladled batter onto the island's built-in griddle and then started turning bacon strips. "What do you need to know?"

"You heard about Tony Vargas being murdered, right?"

"I did, but what does that have to do with you? This isn't your territory anymore."

"The main suspect is an old friend of mine."

"O'Rourke?" Frank frowned at her. "You've kept up with Dermot O'Rourke since he turned in his collar? That's gotta be what? Ten years?"

"Twelve."

Stella tried not to bristle at Frank's tone. Apparently, he didn't approve. But she wasn't a teenager anymore, and he couldn't tell her who she could or couldn't see.

Not that she was *seeing* Dermot in that way.

"I haven't exactly kept up with Dermot, no," she said. "But I knew him pretty well back then. Well enough to know he wouldn't murder anyone."

Mulling that over for a moment as he flipped the first set of pancakes, Frank said, "You'd be surprised what a man will do when cornered."

Though the edge in his tone triggered Stella's curiosity about what he might mean, she kept on track. "Dermot's not that kind of man."

"What kind of man do you think he is?"

"One who is honest, among other things."

Frank barked a laugh. "How about one who can't carry through with his promises. Or maybe he got himself in trouble as a priest and made it out while the going was good. Tony was his altar boy, you know, and with his nose for trouble, he would've known the real scoop."

So the word was out on the street and, despite his protests that he was out of the loop, Frank had tapped right into it. Since there hadn't been an arrest, Dermot's name hadn't yet landed in the tabloids, so the only way Frank could know that the authorities considered Dermot a suspect was via word of mouth. And that had to be via a leak at Area 4.

"Playing the altar boy card isn't fair, Frank," Stella informed him. "There was never any whisper of scandal in that direction."

"Or maybe you just didn't want to hear it." Frank's brow furrowed for a moment, then softened as he caved. "And maybe you got O'Rourke pinned. Don't mind me. What does an old man know anyhow?"

"You got a coupla good years left in you."

The joke came automatically, but the fact that Frank couldn't dismiss such blatant gossip didn't sit well with Stella. She took a couple of mugs from a shelf and filled them with coffee.

"So, can you get me the word on the street about Tony? I need to know what he was up to."

"Nothing good, I'm sure."

"Just what I'm looking for." She handed Frank his coffee, black, just the way he liked it. "That and some names. Who Tony dealt with since getting out of the joint...who he ticked off lately..."

"I'll see what I can do. Anything else?"

After swallowing a slug of French roast, she said, "Johnny Rincon and Alderman Marta Ortiz."

Frank started. "You mention the two of them in the same breath?"

"Yeah, I do when Tony Vargas is the common denominator."

Wondering if she should tell him about the blackmail aspect of the case, Stella decided not. That information wasn't yet public knowledge, so his having it might put Frank in jeopardy, which was the last thing she wanted.

"Johnny is always up to something," he said, flipping pancakes onto a plate. "Never held down an honest job in his life. I wouldn't put murder past him. But Ortiz is different. The alderman is well respected. High profile."

"And she's a big supporter of Heartland House, so she's involved there. And Tony was her cousin. She had a hand in his parole, but Tony wasn't crazy about her."

"Really?"

Stella was surprised that Frank didn't know. Not that he could be aware of absolutely everything that went on.

"I doubt Marta Ortiz goes around advertising the fact," Stella said. "It wouldn't do her career good to claim a criminal as part of her family, and Tony was bent...well, ever since I can remember. He was Johnny's gofer back in high school." Though Tony probably had been initiated into the gang at an even younger age.

"No good," Frank groused, "the lot of 'em."

"Hey, about that punk on the church steps this morning? What'd he want with you?"

Frank tensed as he piled peaches and pecans on the pancakes. "A job. I need someone to sweep up, run errands, but not anyone that wears colors. I told Falco to clean up and then come see me." He set a plate in front of her. "Here you go, Star, your favorite, just like old times."

Taking a bite, Stella made an enthusiastic sound of appreciation. Frank grinned at her, and she leaned over and kissed his weathered cheek.

"Just like old times," she murmured before stuffing her mouth full.

Stella was glad she'd thought to visit Frank for a variety of reasons.

Now, if only she had some clue as to what he had against Dermot.

DERMOT HAD JUST FINISHED quizzing the night security guard at Heartland about the evening of the murder when the front door slammed and footsteps thundered along the hallway. A disappointed Dermot—he'd gotten no information of value from the man—stepped out of the kitchen to see a large ex-con with wild hair and a full beard heading for the stairs.

His calling out "Bingo Wollensky, freeze!" stopped the guy in his tracks.

One foot on the stairs, Bingo turned, his puffy face pulled into a smile that belied the panic in his eyes. "Hey, Doc, how long you been on the outside?"

"I wasn't arrested. Though maybe you wish I had been."

"Me? No!"

Dermot came closer—and tapping into his past—made his voice low and dangerous, the only thing some of these ex-cons understood. "You pretty much pointed me out to the cops." Fear was a great motivator.

Bingo was visibly starting to sweat. Droplets gathered on his forehead along his prematurely receding hairline.

"Hey, come on, Doc, all I did was pass on what Tony told me."

"What *did* Tony tell you?"

Bingo went wide-eyed. "Nothin' specific! I swear on all that's holy I don't know nothin'!"

Another resident, one Dermot didn't know, entered and grunted as he passed them.

"Maybe this isn't the best place to talk," Dermot said. "Maybe we need someplace more…private."

Bingo began to sweat for real now, droplets running into his eyebrows. "Yeah, yeah, sure, Doc."

But his voice rose nearly to a scared squeak and his eyes looked a little wild—undoubtedly he was contemplating the consequences of being alone with a possible murderer. While Bingo ran numbers and small-time confidence games, he'd never been into violence any more than Tony had.

"Come into my office."

For an office, he'd been assigned the smaller parlor with eight-foot pocket doors, stained-glass-trimmed bay windows and a ceramic-tiled fireplace. In stark contrast, the furniture was secondhand and utilitarian.

"Sit," he told Bingo, who nervously perched on the edge of the threadbare couch. "I wasn't the one who hung Tony from the chandelier like some carnival prize. But someone did. Someone who had easy access to the place."

"I…I just found him is all."

Arms crossed over his chest, Dermot leaned back against the edge of his desk and gave the ex-con what he hoped was a deadly stare. "So, you told the cops you were downstairs when Tony was killed—"

"Watching TV."

"And you didn't hear anything?"

"TV was on loud. I already told the cops," Bingo said. "Twice. I didn't hear nothin' and I didn't see nothin'. I didn't even know you were still here. Cops got that from the guard."

"Let's talk about Tony. You say you passed on what Tony told you to the police, then you say he didn't tell you anything." Dermot gave Bingo an expression of disbelief. "Which of these is true?"

"You tryin' to confuse me?"

"I'm trying to get to the truth!" Dermot raised his voice in hopes of pushing Bingo even more. "Either Tony told you something or he didn't."

"Tony always h-had s-secrets," Bingo said. "Sometimes he'd just bait you to get you interested, then he'd back off and not really tell you d-details you could get a h-handle on."

In Dermot's experience, the dead man had liked to talk, whether it was to brag or to confess—or maybe that was just with someone who couldn't pass on information that could get him in trouble. Though Tony hadn't come through with anything substantive about the blackmail in their sessions, Dermot thought he might have eventually.

If he hadn't been murdered first.

"So Tony baited you about me?" he asked Bingo. "He said we shared some kind of secret?"

"Yeah, from way back when he knew you before. Don't worry, though." Fear oozed off Bingo again. His whole face was damp with sweat. "I couldn't squeal nothin' to the cops, 'cause I don't know nothin'. See?"

Dermot wanted to grab him by the front of his shirt

and demand to know why Bingo couldn't simply keep his own counsel. He sucked in a deep breath and reminded himself that he was not into violence.

As for Bingo, like Tony, the big man suffered from low self-esteem. Having something to tell the cops probably had made him feel important at the moment. Normally Dermot wouldn't categorize Bingo as a squealer, though, so maybe he'd volunteered that information from some long-buried morality, because he really believed Dermot had reason to shut Tony up permanently.

"Tell me more about the secrets." Maybe he could get something there.

"A lot of goofy stuff. But he said he had somethin' on you that you wouldn't want anyone to know. And he was supposed to come into money sometime soon. Big money. Said he just had to play his cards right."

Something Tony never learned to do. No doubt the big money was the blackmail Tony had bragged about in their sessions—probably the very thing that had gotten him killed. Dermot could see how the police had put the two together and come up with him as a potential suspect. But being very familiar with the supposed "secret" he and Tony shared—Tony's last confession to him when he'd been a priest—he knew the authorities weren't going to come up with anything to use against him. At least not anything a prosecutor could use.

Dermot tried again. "So what kind of goofy stuff did Tony brag about?"

"Revenge plots mostly."

"Against?"

"People who screwed him in the past. Like when

he was a kid, this old lady who used to yell at him for running across her lawn…he peed on her grass every night. The yellow spots all over drove her crazy."

Having heard this story himself, Dermot said, "Disgusting but harmless."

"And this chick who wouldn't date him…for weeks he wrote her phone number on the walls in every public bathroom he used."

"Definitely goofy," Dermot agreed, though he'd heard that one before, as well. "Anything a little more serious?"

"Tony talked about pulling one over on someone who'd had some kind of power over him."

"Power?" Dermot sat up and took notice. "What kind of power?"

"That's one of them times when Tony backed off," Bingo said. "All I know is it'd been going on for years, and Tony meant to stop it because he didn't want to be someone's girlfriend in stir again."

Thinking Bingo owed Johnny Rincon a big one for letting him take the fall on that last job they'd pulled, Dermot hoped they might be getting somewhere. "Go on."

"But he didn't have a plan and he only mentioned it that once. I…I just figured he meant you."

"You figured wrong."

No matter how Dermot approached the question, Bingo had no more answers for him, so Dermot dismissed the man with a stern promise to revisit the subject later if necessary. He'd never seen the big ex-con move so fast as he did to get out of that office.

Someone who had power over Tony. Johnny? His cousin Marta? Or someone else?

Throwing himself into the chair behind his desk, Dermot sagged with disappointment. He'd been counting on Bingo knowing more than he had. Hopefully, Stella or Blade was having better luck. Of course, they'd only gotten started, so he couldn't expect too much.

Expectations—his life seemed to be full of them. But usually others expected things of him. This was turnabout time and he wasn't liking it one bit. He found he didn't care to lean on anyone, especially not on Stella.

He'd been everything to her once. Savior. Guardian. Advisor. Now what was he but a burden and possible cause for her dismissal from the CPD?

He could have said no to her offer of help. Could have turned her away. But would she have listened? He guessed that, no matter what, Stella would have put herself in the path of most resistance out of obligation.

He hated being anyone's obligation.

At least this way, in the spirit of cooperation, he had a chance to keep her from sticking her neck out too far for him.

And, a little voice whispered, this way he could be close to her, at least for a while.

Chapter Five

Sixty-eight hours after the estimated time of death and the clock was ticking, Stella thought, as she pushed through the Club Undercover crowd and headed for the bar, where she would rendezvous with Dermot and Blade.

Tonight the neon lights and pounding music simply added to her headache. The farther they got timewise from the murder, the less likely it would be solved. The reality put a lump in her stomach. She only hoped Blade or Dermot himself had gotten something she could run with.

Dermot was already waiting for her at the bar, but he and Blade looked all too serious when they spotted her.

Her spirits fell further. Undoubtedly, they'd had no more luck than she.

"Aren't we a cheerful group," she muttered, sliding onto the stool next to Dermot.

"Tell us something that'll put a smile on our faces."

"My cousin Frank agreed to see what he could find out about Tony's activities and associates."

Unfortunately, no one else she'd talked to that afternoon had been of any help.

"So will Leroy," Blade said. "He'll keep his ear to the ground to see if Johnny had Tony involved in anything underhanded."

Stella knew Leroy—a mechanic who had at one time worked for Frank—and his cousin Carla, who'd been married to Johnny until she'd had enough of his physical abuse. Leroy was nothing if not loyal to family and therefore wanted to see Johnny get what he deserved.

Remembering that Leroy had not only a wife but five kids to worry about, Stella said, "You did tell him to keep a low profile, right?"

Who knew what form Johnny's revenge would take if he suspected the man was working against him.

"Leroy's smarter than he seems," Blade said. "He'll be careful."

How she hated involving civilians, Stella thought. Bad enough that she'd introduced Dermot to Team Undercover. Not that some of them couldn't handle themselves—Logan and Blade at least had experience with violence. But Cass could become a target. Or Gabe. Or Gideon himself. Both men had that edge that indicated they could be tough when necessary, but she didn't know that firsthand.

Trying to shake the negativity, she asked Dermot, "What about you?"

"I spent some time at the halfway house. Everyone there seems to be deaf, dumb and blind."

"So you got nothing?"

"Next to nothing. Bingo Wollensky said Tony was

trying to get out from under someone's thumb before he landed in jail again.''

"Back to Johnny Rincon," Blade said. "If he was planning something big that involved Tony, Leroy will find out."

"What about your session notes?" she asked Dermot. "Did you get to them?"

"I did. Tony complained about a lot of his acquaintances, but no one in particular—other than Marta Ortiz, that is. I looked over all the entries about her more closely. What I got was his cousin wanted him to do something he didn't. Nothing specific that would help us, of course. He hated the pressure and was afraid that if he caved, he'd end up on the short end of the stick. If that makes sense."

Stella said, "That could mean—"

"That it was Marta's thumb Tony was trying to get out from under, not Johnny's."

"But he was afraid of jail time," Blade said. "So that part doesn't make sense."

"Not yet," Stella said. "But if there's something there, we'll get to it."

It all had to make sense eventually, or Dermot would end up behind bars for something he didn't do.

A HALF HOUR LATER and no lightbulbs turned on for any of them. Now business had picked up and Blade was busy trying to keep up with customer demand.

Dermot supposed he should call it quits and usher Stella home, then try to get a good night's sleep himself, but he wasn't ready to call it a night yet, not when he could spend time in her company.

"Time to get closer, boys and girls," the deejay

said in a low, sexy voice. "And 'Say Yes' with Floetry."

The music smoothed out to slow and sexy, and Dermot couldn't help himself. Sliding off his stool, he held out his hand. "Dance?"

Stella's eyes widened slightly as did her lips. Luscious lips, he thought, wanting more than anything to taste them. Well, maybe not more than anything. Each part of her was more tempting than the next, and he wanted to taste every inch of her beautiful body.

"Why not," she said softly, giving him her hand.

His gut tightened as he led her to the dance floor. He'd imagined her in his arms so many times…her in his arms when she wasn't wounded and hurting, that was.

Dermot couldn't believe how right Stella felt pressed up against him. She fit him perfectly, as if they'd been made to go together.

If only…

Her hair was soft around her face, loosely clipped up in back. The hairstyle and the wide-necked rust sweater she wore accentuated the length of her neck.

He moved his head in closer to hers and inhaled her light spicy scent—ginger, maybe—and thought how that suited her personality. Definitely spicy. Though she'd been violated, she'd come back fighting. He'd watched her grow and bloom before his eyes. Considering what had happened to her, she'd seemed a miracle to him.

If only…

For a moment he let his mind drift and his body respond to hers. He closed his eyes and he could see them joined together, their movements against each other fiercely passionate. He'd had this fantasy many times before, and now the image seemed as right as the two of them on the dance floor.

Then the sultry song ended and the deejay's voice whispered across the floor and Stella's eyes widened as if she'd just woken up from a dream.

Exactly how he was feeling.

"Again?" he asked.

Though she looked tempted, she shook her head and her voice was a choked whisper. "Once was enough...."

Once would never be enough for him, but Dermot didn't know if he could ever tell her that.

There were other things he couldn't tell her, as well. Things about the past.

The seal of the confessional would haunt him always.

The next set started with J.Lo's "I'm Glad," and couples wound in each other's arms surrounded them as they made their way off the dance floor. A few were kissing, others were enjoying each other's bodies a little too intimately for such a public arena.

More than enough hormones to set the place on fire, Dermot thought....

His among them.

This wouldn't work, he told himself. Much as he might be tempted, he couldn't be with Stella. So why was he torturing himself?

When they returned to the bar area, Gideon and the other members of Team Undercover were the only people there. Cass was setting fluted wineglasses in a row, and Blade was filling them with champagne.

Not wanting anyone here to read his mind, to know

what was rolling around in his psyche, Dermot made certain to keep a little distance from Stella.

"It's Logan's last night working here." Gideon handed a glass to Logan and Gabe, then to Dermot and Stella. "I thought we'd send him off with a toast." He lifted his glass: "To a dedicated security chief and loyal friend, John Logan. May your return to the Chicago Police Department be the journey you imagine it will be."

"Here, here," the others murmured, all sipping their champagne.

"And to Gabriel Conner. I know we couldn't find a better man to take Logan's place."

"I'd pass the baton if I had one," Logan told Gabe.

The tiny lines around Gabe's green eyes crinkled as he lifted his glass. "I just hope I do half the job you've done at the club…and otherwise."

Dermot figured Gabe meant on Team Undercover. They all took another sip. Then they were laughing and talking. All but Cass. He caught her staring at him, her expression intense. Great. Exactly what he'd been trying to avoid. The blue neon of the bar seemed to surround her like an aura as their gazes locked. Then Cass's expression smoothed—he swore he recognized empathy before she turned to her friends.

But Dermot felt as if he'd been kicked in the gut. Part of him imagined Cass had been rooting around inside his head as if trying to read what was there. Of course, that was ridiculous. An overactive imagination. Even so, his pulse went ragged until he took a deep, calming breath.

"Should we open another bottle?" Cass asked.

"No more for me. I'm driving," Stella said, setting her half-empty glass on the bar.

Dermot did likewise. "Same here."

He felt a little light-headed but not from the champagne. Stella did that to him every time he was around her.

Gideon leaned in to Dermot and softly said, "We're doing what we can to help you, but so far we've come up with blanks. Maybe that'll change tomorrow with Logan installed back in Area 4."

"If anyone will talk to him."

"No one in that office or in the neighborhood knows about his connections. Except maybe Johnny Rincon, since he was involved in our last case. He's seen us all. But he's the kind of man who makes a point of *not* talking to anyone in authority—well, not if he can help it."

Dermot nodded. "I appreciate whatever you can do."

Really, he didn't have a whole lot of faith that a bunch of strangers could clear him. But the simple fact that they were on his side, and willing to do what they could, kept him in a more positive frame of mind. He glanced at Cass and wished he could read *her* mind.

Suddenly leaning into him, Stella murmured, "I'm ready to call it a night."

He was, too, if that meant he could be alone with her. "I'll see you home."

"I have my car."

"Then I'll follow you."

"That's not necessary."

"I want to."

Her lips parted again…and then closed. Either she couldn't think of another argument or she'd decided to give it up. Maybe she wanted him to follow her…to see her inside…to…

Dermot stopped himself before he got carried away.

STELLA COULDN'T SETTLE DOWN on the drive home. All the way, she kept checking her rearview mirror to see the lights behind her that never wavered.

Why had Dermot insisted on following her home, as though she needed to be protected? She was a cop, better prepared to take care of herself than he was.

She had mixed feelings about his concern for her. Partly it felt good—like old times without the psychological load. But the other part felt like a mistake, like letting him do for her would send her hurtling back to the past, so she didn't know what to think as she parked her car in front of her building.

Dermot pulled up at the curb right behind her.

They met on the parkway beneath a maple that hadn't yet given up its leaves. The night air was nippy, yet she felt warm from the inside out.

"Thanks for seeing me home."

"My pleasure."

"Your pleasure to drive six miles out of your way." There was an edge to her voice she couldn't help. "Six miles in each direction."

"My pleasure comes from seeing you home safely, no matter the distance."

She arched her eyebrows at him and tartly said, "I'm the one carrying the gun."

"Excuse me? I don't believe I came across a weapon on the dance floor."

Going tight inside at the reminder of how close they'd gotten, if only for a few minutes on a dance floor—of how deeply that closeness had affected her—Stella said, "Seriously, I'm carrying."

Dermot stepped toward her and slid his hands around her waist. "Where?" His thumbs hooked under the edge of her sweater and tracked light lines along her flesh.

Stella shuddered at the exquisite sensation that spread and quickly multiplied. She knew she ought to stop this before it went any further.

"Wrong part of the anatomy," she said, strangely breathless. "Try an ankle holster."

Even though she knew she ought to break away and go inside—like right this second!—Stella was caught by the magic of the moment. Her hands rested lightly against Dermot's chest. Against the tender flesh of her palms, his heartbeat quickened and strengthened as they stood together as one.

As she'd always wanted them to be, Stella thought. Only, before, together had been unthinkable. But what about now? Now seemed…different…and yes, possible.

Her heart quickened. "Dermot…"

"Star…"

Their murmurs twined together and faded off as their lips met. Stella didn't know who kissed whom. They were on the same wavelength, acting together.

Dermot deepened the kiss, twining his tongue with hers. It was a long, hot kiss that had every part of her trembling with need. When it was over, she nipped his lower lip and kissed him again. Then he pulled her hard against him, and she slid her arms up around his neck. His hand found the side of her breast, and the sensation of his touch weakened her knees so that she leaned hard into him.

They couldn't be closer, unless...

The thought of being naked with him, of feeling his skin sliding against hers, of him sliding in and out of her, inspired both desire and fear.

Freaked more than a little, Stella tore her mouth from Dermot's. She placed her hands between them and shoved at his chest. He didn't resist her but stepped back. They stood there, staring at each other, both breathing hard.

"Star—"

"I should go upstairs. Now."

"I'll walk you—"

"No! I mean, I'm fine!" she said, knowing she sounded waspish. "I've held you up long enough. You should go home now!"

His expression closed and his spine straightened. "Fine. Tomorrow, then."

"Tomorrow will be a better day," she muttered, a little embarrassed. "We'll get a lead on the murder. Gut feeling. Cop thing."

Stella didn't know what else to say, so she backed off. She had to force herself not to run. Her pulse was jagging, but not a good sensation.

What had she been thinking? she asked herself, taking the front steps two at a time. No matter her affection for Dermot, she couldn't get too personally involved with him.

Couldn't. Shouldn't. Wouldn't.

Not that she had some reason for not getting involved with a man. Some other man.

Just not him.

She slipped her keys from her pocket and made it inside in record time. But then, in the vestibule, she fumbled getting the inside door unlocked.

Dermot had seen her at her weakest moment. He'd picked her up off the alley pavement and had covered her naked body...had tended to her wounds himself when she wouldn't go to a hospital...had seen each and every physical mark that bastard Lamey had left on her.

And she, in turn, had seen the pity in Dermot's eyes.

She couldn't ever stand to see him look at her like that again.

To her relief, the door finally opened.

Stella took the inside stairs to her second-floor apartment, thinking about how she'd put her rapist in jail for another crime and had gotten herself past the attack. She'd even been with a few men over the years, not that any of those relationships had been serious. Serious had never tempted her. That would entail total trust. In a way, even though she dated and had become intimate with men, the rape was still with her. Probably always would be.

Dermot had seen her naked and bloody...he'd witnessed her humiliation. And even though she had feelings for him, every time she was near him, that memory hovered in the back of her mind.

About to unlock her apartment door, Stella realized a sheet of paper had been wedged between door and jamb.

How had that gotten there? The door at the foot of the stairs had been locked. Then again, that one wasn't a dead bolt, and anyone with a credit card and a little knowledge could have opened it. Stomach tightening, she carefully picked the paper from the door by its edge and flicked it open.

"Bitch," it read in big square letters cut from newspaper headlines and pasted onto a plain piece of paper. "Haven't you learned anything? Stay out of what isn't your concern and stay alive."

DERMOT STILLED THE URGE to punch something as he drove north on Halsted.

Despite the fact that he knew he couldn't get involved with her, Stella was proving to be too much temptation for him. As if his not being able to keep his lips off hers wasn't bad enough, he hadn't been able to keep his hands to himself, either. She'd reacted quickly and had snapped at him, convincing him that she still had issues from the past.

Still shaken by her reaction—obviously he'd gone too far—he only gradually realized another vehicle was following close behind.

The lights on the other vehicle rode too high for a passenger car. An SUV? He squinted into the side-view mirror and saw the outline of a ridiculously large truck. The lights flicked on high a few times, nearly blinding him. Undoubtedly he wasn't going fast enough for the other driver, even though the speed limit was an even thirty.

Grumbling to himself, Dermot sped up only to note that the lights in his rearview mirror didn't get any smaller. Archer Street was directly ahead. Deciding to take the street that angled its way in the general direction of home, he made a fast right.

The truck stayed close behind him.

''What the hell!''

When Dermot sped away without being able to put any distance between him and the truck, he neared his boiling point. He shot under the expressway and zigzagged down a couple of side streets and under the fancy arch that was the official Gateway to Chinatown. Still he couldn't lose the truck. Who the hell was following him? Cops? Or someone who had a different kind of interest in Tony's death?

He had to slow to allow for late-night diners.

A glance in his rearview mirror assured him a bunch of young pedestrians had brought the truck to a stop at last. Dermot saw his chance to escape.

A few more turns took him along a deserted street that backtracked under the expressway in a different location. He sped to the viaduct, but then slowed there and pulled to the far right, parking up against the foundation, where he cut his engine and lights.

Seconds later, familiar brights cut a swath through the night as the truck swept by him. Dermot got only a fast look. Black. A Ford, he thought. License plates XO 74 something.

Not that he intended to report it. The police only wanted to hear one thing from him, and that was a confession. So why had he been followed? he wondered. The pursuit had been too focused, too intense to believe he'd been a random playmate.

What, then? Dermot wondered.

He was still thinking of it several minutes later, when he started his engine, made a U-turn and headed for home.

THE DEATH THREAT floated from her fingers, and Stella went for her ankle holster. Within seconds she was armed, her snub-nosed revolver in hand. So the killer already knew she was on his or her trail. Her heart was pounding so hard she could hear her pulse wash through her head.

Was whoever had left the warning still around?

She wasn't about to go outside and find out. But what about inside?

Stella tried her front door. When it didn't open, she took a calming breath. Even so, after unlocking the door, she cautiously slipped into the apartment and turned on the lights in every room, all the while ready to take on anyone waiting to attack her.

The apartment was empty.

She sagged with relief.

What to do?

If she reported the threat, she would be in trouble with the department. Mack would rescind her comp time until further notice and would forbid her from continuing with her private investigation. Her involvement would become a department matter, maybe the start of the end of her career.

"Damn it!"

Slipping the paper into a plastic zipper bag, Stella decided to give it to Logan. Now that he was back in the department, he could have it run for prints.

Wanting in the worst way to call Dermot and tell him they had the killer nervous, Stella knew that was the last thing she should do. If Dermot knew she'd been threatened, he would refuse her help, and she couldn't have that.

She couldn't rely on a weapon at her ankle, either. From now on, she would be properly armed.

Suddenly it struck her.

…haven't you learned anything…

Her heart started to pound once more. Unless she was mistaken, that was a reference to the rape meant to shut her up. Twelve years ago she'd had information about some burglaries she'd meant to give to the police. The rape had been her punishment. And if she were to report the assault to the police, the rapist had threatened that her younger sister would have been next.

But now her rapist was in jail.

That meant someone other than Dermot knew what had happened to her all those years ago.

Tony's murderer?

Was there a connection?

Chapter Six

As if he knew she was coming, Rick Lamey stepped out of the alleyway and stopped directly in front of her, blocking her path. "Where you think you're goin', Star?"

"Home." She'd just left Candera's Mercado where she'd bought milk and bread. Warily, she eyed the gang member with the meanest reputation in the neighborhood and said, "Get outta my way."

"You think you can tell me what to do, bitch?"

With that he crowded her straight into the alley. Heart thumping, trying not to panic, she stumbled backward but caught herself before she fell.

"C'mon, Rick, let me alone. My ma's waiting for me and I'm late already."

"She's gonna have to wait a while longer." He whipped out a knife.

Her mouth went dry and her fingers went numb and her bag slipped from her fingers to crash against the alley pavement. Something wet splashed against her legs...the milk. She backed up farther, trying to keep a safe distance between them. If there was any such *thing as safe where he and the other members of the Vipers were concerned.*

"What is it you want, Rick? I don't have much money, but—"

His laugh sent a chill up her spine.

"I don't want your money, bitch. I'm gonna teach you a lesson you ain't gonna forget."

Then, before she could make a break for it, he grabbed her arm, whipped her around and dragged her farther from the street. She struggled, tried to fight, but she didn't know how and she was no match for his strength. A quarter of the way down the alley, he threw her to the pavement where he knelt on her chest and pricked her neck with the knife tip.

She tried to scream but nothing came out. And then he slapped her hard.

"That's for sticking your nose in our business. You ain't gonna tell the pigs nothin'," he whispered. "When I'm through with you, you'll wish you never thought of squealing."

With the knife still at her throat, he backed off enough so he could tear at her clothing.

A shrill scream echoed through her head...

Dark memories threatening to smother her, Stella popped straight up in bed and struggled to find her breath. Her heart was beating too fast, too hard, just as it had on that fateful night.

Only, it was morning now. Present day. Bright sunlight streamed in her twin windows and danced along the creamy gold walls.

The phone rang...and she recognized the shrill scream of her awful dream. The ringing had saved her from experiencing the full horror of the nightmare that she hadn't had in years. No doubt the new threat had prompted its revival. Hand trembling, wondering who might be calling her so early, she reluctantly picked up the receiver.

"Hello?"

"Star? You sound a little strange," came a familiar voice filled with concern. "Did I interrupt something?"

"Frank. No, nothing. I was sleeping."

"Sorry. Go on back to sleep. We'll talk later."

"No, I'm awake now."

She didn't want to go back to sleep…to dream…to relive the worst night of her life, something she hadn't done in the last decade.

So why now?

Then she remembered the note…

"So what's the word on the street, Frank?"

Throwing her legs over the edge of the bed, she stretched and pushed the past back where it belonged, at least for the moment. Despite the threat, she had to be objective. She knew that. She just had to figure out how.

"Louie Z.," he said.

Shocked—Luis Zamora was another cop from the old neighborhood—Stella asked, "Why? What did you hear?"

"That he was on Tony like white on rice. They had a hate-hate relationship going on."

Stella slid out of bed, and with her free hand straightened the hibiscus-red and spice-gold water-color linens, a little extravagance that made her hand-me-down bedroom furniture appear more luxurious.

"Cops don't like criminals in general. And Luis

was the cop who sent Tony up for the burglary charges, so of course they didn't play nice together.''

"But apparently this particular cop likes Johnny Rincon well enough to play poker with *him* over at Skipper's.''

Now that got her attention. "I thought Luis was through with Johnny.''

"Apparently not. Who knows what he's doing for his old pal.''

If Luis was truly friends with Johnny again, that would be something of a bombshell, Stella thought.

Back in high school, Luis Zamora—then known as Louie Z.—had been Johnny's best friend and a member of the Vipers. After graduation, Luis literally had to fight his way out of the gang. Then he'd severed his friendship with Johnny and had turned his life around, going to the community college and then the academy. She'd been in the same class with him. Not that they'd been friends even then.

"I hope you're wrong about Luis.'' She dreaded hearing about another cop gone bad. "Maybe it's only poker.''

"Yeah, you could be right. A cop with a yen to gamble mixing it up with a known criminal, if one who hasn't spent more than a few days in lock-up— yeah, that could be innocent enough.''

Of course it didn't sound innocent, and Stella knew she would have to find out for herself. Though Johnny had been arrested on several occasions, he always managed to slip through the system. It had never occurred to her before that he might have help from the inside…

"Thanks, Frank. I knew I could count on you to come through for me."

"We're family. I hope you'll always remember that."

Guilt prompted her to say, "All right, I get the message. I promise not to neglect you because of work."

"You can always come to me, Star, with any problem."

For a moment she thought to tell Frank about the note, then decided against it. Nothing he could do about it but worry.

"And as for this thing," Frank continued, "I'm not done on my end."

Stella laughed. "Sounds like you're getting into playing detective."

"I have hidden talents you don't know about."

Wondering what they might be, she decided to leave it a mystery. "Thanks again for the lead."

"My pleasure. Keep in touch."

"Will do."

Stella hung up and headed for the bathroom and the shower.

Louie Z. Surely he wasn't involved with his old gang. But how to find out for certain?

Stella was thinking about it as she prepared a simple breakfast of low-fat cottage cheese and peaches. Of course! Logan. She ate with one hand, punched in the Area 4 number on her telephone with the other.

But when Logan got on the line, he didn't give her a chance to tell him about Luis Zamora.

"How did you hear?" he asked.

"Hear what?"

He lowered his voice. "Norelli and Walker brought Dermot in again for further questioning."

"Any idea of why?"

"No other suspects."

"Is he alone?" she asked.

"Not this time. He brought Avery Stark with him."

"Good. I'm on my way."

Not that she had a plan. She figured she would simply hang around and improvise.

But mere moments after stepping foot in Area 4, she spotted Luis Zamora deep in conversation with another officer dressed in plain clothes.

What was he doing here? Stella wondered. He worked out of District 12, the same as she had before her promotion.

He sat on the desk and leaned over, his head close to the woman's. With his dark good looks and dimpled chin, he was charming the desk dolly, who seemed to be doing most of the talking.

About what? The Vargas case?

Then he chucked the female officer under the chin, dropped a folder on her desk—no doubt delivering papers on a case being the reason he was here in the first place—then straightened to leave. And made direct eye contact with Stella. He looked away first and headed for the front door, where she hurriedly intercepted him.

"Luis. It's been a while."

"Stella."

His tone was cool, and he seemed about to push past her but she kept in his way and put a staying hand on his arm.

"We need to talk."

His jaw clenched, hardening his features. "I only got a minute."

"Then we'll talk fast." She hooked a hand in the crook of his elbow and pulled him out of the line of traffic.

"About?"

"Tony Vargas."

"I don't get it."

"I understand you had a coupla run-ins with him shortly before he was offed."

His eyes narrowing, he asked, "You got a point here?"

She shrugged. "I thought maybe you knew what he was up to."

"If I knew he was up to no good, I would've arrested him."

Did Luis sound defensive or was she imagining it?

"So you were what…" Stella asked. "Hassling him to keep him straight?"

Luis's jaw worked and he took a deep breath before asking, "What're you suggesting, Stella?"

She gave him an innocent shrug. "Just trying to get the facts to help a friend."

"I think that detective's star has gone to your head. Or maybe the suspect has gotten to something more personal," he said.

Heat searing her at his obvious implication, Stella didn't try to stop Luis when he moved away from her and made for the exit. She was too busy wondering why he was so defensive. At least he didn't call her any of the names that no doubt tempted him—women on the force too often put up with verbal abuse from male cops. Did Luis really have something to hide or did he simply resent her questioning him?

"Anything?" came a low voice from behind her as Logan sauntered by and stopped at a nearby drinking fountain.

She got behind him as if she, too, were thirsty. "Just more questions."

"Stark was making…a big noise…when I went by the interrogation room," he said of Dermot's lawyer between sips.

"Frank gave me a lead. Luis Zamora didn't like Tony. I just saw him and tried to find out why. He gave me the brush-off."

"I'll dig around some." Logan straightened and said, "Dermot should be out of there any minute now."

"One more thing." Stella slipped him the plastic bag containing the warning she'd gotten the night before. "Someone doesn't want me on this case. Have the lab check for fingerprints. And don't say a word to Dermot."

"Stella—"

But another detective was coming down the hall, so Logan slid the note into his pocket and casually moved away from the fountain.

Stella nodded and stooped to take a sip. Then, thinking she ought to hook up with Dermot outside where she wouldn't ruffle any more feathers than she already had, she left the building and leaned against the trunk of a tree in the parkway.

The wait wasn't long, less than twenty minutes. And Dermot left the building alone. His lawyer must have had other business.

"Dermot, over here," she said with a wave.

Stella's mouth went dry as she watched Dermot walk toward her, his expression serious. And why not—he had reason to fear being railroaded. He was suited up today, and the expensive, tailored look fit him perfectly. Hell, anything would look good on him…nothing at all would look even better.

Telling herself to keep it in check, she stepped out to the sidewalk.

Dermot stopped directly in front of her, so close that his heat lit her from the inside out, exactly the way it had when they'd kissed the night before.

"How did it go?" she choked out.

If he caught her nervousness, he didn't show it.

"Better than I expected, thanks to that lawyer you got me. They dragged me in to ask about the velvet ropes again—they keep coming back to two being stolen when only one was found with Tony, as if I kept the second one for my next victim. Stark knows what he's doing," Dermot admitted, his gaze narrowing on her. "This isn't a coincidence—your being here this morning, I mean."

"No, Logan alerted me. Instinct. I got here before I thought it through."

"Well, then, having someone working on the inside appears to be a good thing."

"Not that my coming down here actually accomplished anything." Other than pissing off Luis Zamora.

"You brightened my day."

She couldn't help her reaction to his words. Her pulse fluttered and her mouth curved into a smile. "Well, it was worth the trip, then. And as long as no one links Logan with me, he should be able to squeeze whatever information there is to be had from Norelli and Walker.''

And get an ID on those fingerprints. She knew she ought to be open with Dermot about last night, but she didn't want to start the day with him ordering her to back off. Telling him could wait.

"What now?" Dermot asked. "I assume you dropped whatever you were doing to rush down here and be my moral support."

"Frank handed me a lead this morning. I thought I would follow that up."

"Could you use some company?"

"If you're the company, absolutely."

Truth be told, she would take any company she could get after that morning's nightmare. She hadn't been back to Candera's Mercado since the night of her rape, and she wouldn't be going there now if it wasn't for Dermot.

They took both of their cars and met on 18th Street within view of the el station with its ethnic murals, public artwork being an integral part of the neighborhood.

As they walked down the block together, Dermot took her arm. His fingers through her jacket were firm and telegraphed a sensual message she figured he didn't mean to all parts of her body. Stella tried to relieve her growing tension—not only because of him being so close, but because of where they were—by reiterating Frank's phone call and her fruitless chat with Luis Zamora.

"So now I've alerted a potential suspect," she said,

on alert for anything out of place around her. "And if he has something to hide, he'll bury it."

"If he can. And if he has something to worry about, he might just get sloppy."

"We can hope."

Stella noted the mostly Mexican neighborhood was already prepared for the Day of the Dead, which combined indigenous Mexican and Catholic beliefs. Though officially celebrated on the first two days of November, the Mexican Fine Arts Museum down the street sponsored an extended celebration, beginning before Halloween. The celebration wasn't morbid, but one that invoked humor and that honored deceased ancestors. Two- and three-dimensional skeletons decorated shop windows, and bakeries and small stores sold bread and candy skulls.

When they got within sight of Candera's Mercado, Stella slowed down. "I thought I would check in with Señora Candera. She always did like to talk. And she's friends with Luis's mother."

Dermot echoed, "Candera...I don't remember her."

"But she might remember you, even if you didn't hear her confession. Maybe you ought to keep to the background while I see what I can find out."

He could watch her back, Stella thought, even knowing her nerves were for nothing. No one would dare follow up on that threat she'd received the night before, not now when she was a cop.

As they entered Candera's Mercado, which specialized in Mexican imports and produce used in neighborhood ethnic kitchens, Stella wondered if Dermot remembered that this was the store where she'd picked up her groceries that fateful night of her attack.

A string of paper skeletons danced among the garlic and peppers overhead. Stella stopped at the fresh fruit counter and bagged a few mangoes, stalling to get her nerves in check. She glanced sideways at Dermot, who was studying a shelf of imported canned products and keeping his back to the counter. Taking a steadying breath, she headed for the register, where—dressed in widows' weeds as she had been for as long as Stella could remember—Señora Candera sat reading a novella, a Spanish-language romance comic book.

"Señora Candera, how are you today?"

"Estrella," she said, using the Spanish version of Stella's name. Peering at her through thick glasses, the older woman smiled and set down her story. "It's been so long since I see you. I hear you make detective. I always knew you'd be important someday."

Stella's answering smile felt a little stiff. "I thought you said I would get married and have fine babies."

"That, too. You're still young."

"Not feeling so young right now."

"The work is hard, yes?"

"One particular case." She handed the store owner a five-dollar bill. "Tony Vargas."

Señora Candera hurriedly crossed herself and mumbled something in Spanish. Stella only caught the "poor Tony" part. Not that she was glad to see him dead, yet there had been nothing poor about Tony but his bank account. He'd been a criminal and all-round weasel as Stella remembered him. But of course she wouldn't go into that.

Instead she sighed sympathetically and said, "If only we could find his killer."

"I hear they have a suspect." Señora Candera rang up the mangoes on her register. "That ex-priest. The Irish one."

As if there had been more than one in the neighborhood.

Stella confided, "He was set up," and surreptitiously glanced at Dermot who was within earshot now, though his back was still turned.

"Really?"

Stella nodded. "Maybe you can help, Señora Candera. If you could tell me who Tony got friendly with after he made parole and came back to the neighborhood…"

"I only saw him a few times, and always he was alone. But maybe I can ask Carmen Zamora. She said Luis had some personal business with Tony."

Carmen being Luis's mother, Stella remembered. "When was that?"

"Not long ago." The store owner carefully counted out the change, which Stella shoved into her jacket pocket. "Maybe a week or so."

"You wouldn't know what kinda business?"

The woman shrugged. "Something about big money."

Wondering if Señora Candera knew more, Stella picked up her purchase and left her card with her cell number on the counter. "If you think of anything, you give me a call."

The woman nodded. "And you, Estrella, don't be such a stranger."

Stella turned to signal Dermot but he'd disappeared. She found him waiting for her outside, out of sight of the store windows.

By way of explanation, he said, "I figured if I stayed longer without buying anything, I would look pretty suspicious. So, what juicy offering did the good señora have for you?" he asked as they moved down the street and he slipped a hand around her waist.

A thrill shot through her, straight to her knees. Could he possibly know what he was doing to her? Stella wondered, trying to remain natural around him.

"Señora Candera told me Luis had some business with Tony that involved big money."

"The blackmail?"

"Maybe...or maybe it's just poker," she joked, trying to keep from thinking about Dermot in a more personal way.

"What about poker?"

"Something Frank told me this morning—that Luis plays poker with Johnny Rincon over at Skipper's, and I thought maybe Tony did, too."

"Odd...I wonder..."

"What?"

"When I was grilling Bingo Wollensky, he mentioned Tony was due for big money, then said something about playing his cards right. What if he meant that literally, as in a poker game?"

"Things are starting to come together," she muttered, her thoughts suddenly spinning so fast that she almost ran down another woman walking in the other direction. "Sorry," she gasped when she saw who it was.

Alderman Marta Ortiz looked nothing like her late cousin. While Tony had shown every bit of his Mex-

ican heritage through his bronzed skin and broad
cheekbones, Marta was almost fair by comparison,
and her features were more delicate. She was also tall
for a Latina, and her heels made her equal in height
to Stella so she could look her in the eyes. Now there
was the resemblance to Tony, Stella thought—the
eyes, deep-set, dark and piercing.

"Detective Jacobek, what a surprise to see you
here," the alderman said. "Considering you don't
work this district anymore."

"I'm afraid we haven't met."

Which, in truth, they hadn't, though Stella had seen
the other woman in the neighborhood, had even
worked details around her while still in uniform.

"Let's not play games. You know who I am. You
know Tony Vargas was my cousin." Marta's sharp
gaze shifted to Dermot, but she kept talking to Stella.
"And I know who *he* is. You've picked the wrong
side to work on, *chica.*"

"You're not interested in justice?"

The alderman's gaze whipped back to Stella's.
"Watch your mouth!"

Starting, Stella asked, "Or?"

"You'll find that my influence is widespread."

"One of Tony's major complaints about you,"
Dermot said.

Marta blinked and opened her mouth, but before
she could conjure a retort, Stella said, "Tony was
afraid of you, Alderman Ortiz. Why was that?"

"You dare to question me?"

"Are you above the law?"

Marta flinched as if hit. "You'll see that it doesn't
pay to cross me, Detective."

And with that she stalked off, leaving Stella steaming and staring after her. "She certainly has an inflated ego."

"If that's all it is," Dermot said.

"What do you mean?"

"You wouldn't consider the alderman's appearance a little too convenient, would you?"

"Her office *is* on the next block," Stella told him in an attempt to rationalize. But Marta Ortiz was the one person Tony had harped on in his sessions with Dermot. "Then again, if someone spotted us and made a quick call…"

"She decided to issue a warning in person," Dermot finished. "Goes to character."

Her appearance did seem too convenient, Stella admitted. "The interesting part is that you weren't a surprise to her. She knew I was helping you. I wonder who took the pains to tell her."

"Her influence is widespread, remember," Dermot said, reiterating the woman's words.

"At least as far as Area 4."

No doubt the alderman had been in touch with Detectives Norelli and Walker. But would they give her the lowdown on another officer's activities? Not a good thing. Usually those on the job closed ranks against the outside and kept their internal beefs internal. But first Frank had found out Dermot was the only suspect, and now Marta Ortiz knew Stella was helping him.

Having a big, fat leak made Stella distinctly uneasy.

And reminded her of the personal threat if she continued helping Dermot. She only hoped whoever had left that note for her had been sloppy enough to leave his—or her—calling card in the way of fingerprints. Maybe then they'd get to the truth of the matter.

"Are you okay?"

Realizing Dermot was frowning at her, she said, "It's not me you should be worrying about." Not unless he was psychic. "I was just fixated."

One eyebrow raised in question. "If you say so. What next?"

Her stomach growled, reminding her that it had been hours since she'd eaten. "Lunch, I guess."

Brain food might give her a clue as to how to proceed from there.

AFTER LUNCH they made a few more stops along 18th Street and on some of the side streets, talking to businesspeople and long-term residents about Tony Vargas. Who might have seen him…who he was with…what rumors they might have heard. Stella hadn't expected much, and indeed, they came up empty. Even so, she tried to put on a good face for Dermot's sake.

"Things are coming together," she said as they exited yet another store. "We just gotta figure out how."

"Nice that you've developed an optimistic streak."

"You should, too. You have the best on your side."

"I know you are."

"I wasn't shining my own buttons. You have a whole team working to find the truth."

And enough time had passed that maybe Logan had a piece of it. Stella wanted in the worst way to call him to find out, but she couldn't do it in front of Dermot. If he knew about the threat, he might refuse her further help.

"I'm about done in for the day," she said. "I think I'll go home for a shower and some downtime, and meet you back at the club later."

"Sounds like a plan," he agreed. "I have another stop I want to make before heading home, but I can walk you to your car first."

"Doesn't sound like it's on your way. So go."

Dermot gave her shoulders a squeeze. "Thanks for everything, Star."

If he really wanted to thank her, he could do better than that. Stella thought. But then, she shouldn't be looking for trouble. Kissing him the night before had blown her mind and not only in a good way.

"Later," she said, backing up.

He backed away, too, then he waved her off and turned away. Wondering where he was going—and why she hadn't asked—she watched him for longer than she should have before heading for her car.

Swinging the bag of mangoes, Stella sauntered down the block, thinking of Dermot. Of them.

Of the possibilities.

Were they possible as a couple?

Her heart said yes, but tough as she might have become on the outside, inside she was scared. Could he ever look at her as a woman without seeing the violated young parishioner he'd picked up off the pavement? She couldn't stand it if he ever looked at her with pity again.

She turned the corner where her car was parked and came face-to-face with another reason to be afraid. The teenage punk was about five feet, ten inches of pure threat, draped in oversize khakis, a long-sleeved T-shirt imprinted with a snake design and a green bandanna around his forehead.

"Hey, *chica*, what you got for me?"

For a moment Stella felt faint. She started to back up and realized the punk was looking over her shoulder. She chanced a quick glance back and saw the first one's companions, younger and smaller but no less venomous, blocking her way.

Three Vipers, and one of her.

Her world tilted, and the bag of mangoes dropped from nerveless fingers and hit the pavement with a splat....

Chapter Seven

Every time Dermot entered St. Peter's, the past came back to bite him. He stood there at the back of the church for a moment, allowing his eyes to adjust to the dim light. Automatically, they swept across the rows of seats to the confessionals on the east wall. Not in service today, purple velvet roping them off from anyone entering, the confessional booths stood silent sentinel. As silent as one confessor vowed to remain.

"Can I help you?"

Dermot immediately recognized the voice of Father Julio Padilla. He picked him out in the dim light easily, because the priest's once dark hair was now silver. Padilla stood several yards away, his gaze focused in the same direction Dermot's had been—on the confessionals. Or perhaps on the velvet ropes themselves. He couldn't believe Dermot had stolen the bizarre murder weapon, could he? Someone must have believed it or the detectives couldn't have put the coincidence together so fast—his having been in this church the same night the velvet ropes had come up missing. Odd that only one had been used and the other was still gone.

"Are you here to make your confession, my son?"

"Don't be shy, Father. Go ahead and ask if I murdered Tony Vargas."

"Did you?"

Dermot couldn't believe the man who'd put him on the right path…who he'd worked under for more than a year…who was his confessor…had to ask.

"No. I might have thought to do Tony violence once years ago, but I didn't kill him. That doesn't seem to matter. Unless I can find a way to clear my name…"

Father Padilla gravely inclined his head. "I see. Come into the office where we can speak in comfort."

Though the priest was small in stature, he had a big presence, just as he always had. He was in his late sixties now, yet his back was still strong and straight, and he walked with the stride of a man far younger. He led the way past side altars with their votives before plaster statues—one of St. Joseph, the other of St. Peter—then around the Blessed Mother and Child to the door to the sacristy, and beyond that, the church office.

While not ornate, the office was comfortable and attractive, from the Oriental carpet to the upholstered couch and chairs to the old wood desk with hand-carved trim.

"Can I get you something, Dermot?" Padilla asked. "Coffee? A soda?"

"The truth would be great. If you have it."

The priest sank behind his desk. His liquid dark

eyes were filled with worry. "Now, what is it you think I can tell you?"

"The word on the street."

Since Father Padilla was a longtime crusader against the gang wars that kept the area dangerous, Dermot figured he would still be a primary source.

"I think you know this, my son."

Trying not to let the fact that people believed he was a murderer get to him, Dermot said, "Below the surface. Who is mourning Tony Vargas?"

The priest shrugged. "As far as I can tell…the man wasn't well liked."

"But was he not well liked by anyone in particular?"

"I think he talked too much for anyone's ease."

"Viper ease." No doubt Tony played with gang secrets to his death.

Padilla inclined his head in agreement.

"Yet Tony took the fall for Johnny Rincon," Dermot went on.

"Probably because Tony preferred life inside to no life at all."

"You're saying he was threatened into taking the fall."

"Most likely. Or paid well for doing so. Or both."

Which meant the priest didn't know for certain. Which meant he hadn't heard the condemning answer in the confessional that Dermot had heard so many years ago.

Paid well…big money… Had Tony been paid or simply been promised a reward when he got back on the outside? How much did Johnny Rincon owe him? *Blackmail money?*

"Does Rincon still run herd on The Vipers?" Dermot asked.

"Once a Viper, always a Viper. But Johnny never called the shots."

"He was their leader for years."

"He was the figurehead. The mouthpiece."

Dermot thought about that. "You're saying someone was pulling his strings?"

"And probably still is."

"Whose strings? Rincon's or the Vipers'?"

"My guess would be both."

"You wouldn't have a name to give me?"

"I'm afraid not."

Even without a name, without an absolute certainty, the speculation put things in a new perspective. Put Tony Vargas's twelve-year-old confession in a new perspective, too.

"I'm sorry I can't be of more help."

"You've already helped, Father, by expanding my thinking. And maybe you can do something more for me."

"If I can."

"Then tell me if you know anything about Tony's blackmail scheme."

Padilla started and said, "You know the seal of the confessional protects him even after death."

Which told Dermot that he'd hit on something. Tony hadn't stopped at taunting Dermot with his blackmail scheme. He'd taken it right from the therapy couch to the confessional. Dermot wondered if Tony had named names. If so, Father Padilla would take them to the grave.

That was the thing about being a priest—no matter

how heinous the crime, repeating any part of a confession under any circumstances was against church canon.

Once the information flowed through the priest to God, it was as good as forgotten.

Only, there were some things a man could never forget.

"HEY, MANNY, big cop is scared," one of the punks behind Stella said.

Breathe, Stella told herself. *Just breathe.*

And think.

She wasn't nineteen and naive any more. She was twice their age and a cop. Trained. Armed. And if she could keep it together mentally and emotionally— dangerous.

She measured the distance to the street, then to her car parked nearby. Even if she had keys in hand so she could beep open the door, she wouldn't make it inside before they got to her. She had no choice but to do something desperate, to turn the tables on them.

Every nerve ready to jump, Stella gazed directly behind her to pick her target. Her choice was obvious. From the looks of the baby gang member, he could be Manny's brother or cousin. He was no more than thirteen or fourteen and hadn't filled out yet.

Not that he couldn't be a killer already, she reminded herself.

What she said was, "You got business with me?"

All the while her heart was thudding against her ribs and she was looking for a way out while keeping her antennae glued to all three punks.

"More like pleasure, *chica*. Another life's lesson for you."

Haven't you learned anything...

The similar words from the note left at her door jolted her to attention. Could it be?

She said, "It takes a man to pleasure a woman and all I see here are little boys with big attitudes."

"*Puta!*" he spat, lunging toward her.

But Stella was faster. She jabbed his chest with a stiff elbow, sidestepped and whirled, one hand whipping under the back of her jacket to her holster. Her hip rammed the slightly built punk off balance, and her free arm snaked around his neck while the other hand brought her gun to his head.

Click...

Safety off.

Everyone froze but Stella, who pulled the stumbling kid away from the others, her gun barrel jammed into his head.

"Stay calm and don't make a move, and nothing will happen to him."

Fury made Manny look even more dangerous, but he didn't budge. His fingers were itching, no doubt to get to his own gun, probably stuck in his waistband under the T-shirt. Only she didn't see any telltale bulge.

"Manny, do something!" the kid squealed.

"You wouldn't shoot Pablo."

Not unless she had to. "You don't know what I would or wouldn't do." She wouldn't be violated again, and she would give them the fight of their short lives if she had to. She tried not to let the idea freak her. She could do this, she told herself and shouted, "Get down on the ground, now!"

Ignoring her command, the third punk circled around behind the leader. "This one's loco, Manny. Leave her be and let's get outta here."

The two older punks started to back up, and the squeeze on Stella's chest eased a little.

His thin body trembling against hers, Pablo asked his *compadres,* "What about me? You can't leave me!"

"She ain't gonna kill no one," Manny said with a sneer. "If she arrests you, you'll get bailed."

With that, the two older boys fled, and Stella's knees went weak with relief as she lowered her gun arm. But when the kid tried to free himself, she shoved his slight body face-flat against the building where she patted him down. No weapons. Maybe Manny didn't trust him with a gun or knife. Good choice. But if Manny or the other punk had been carrying, she hadn't spotted any telltale bulge.

Stella grabbed Pablo's shoulder and flipped him so that his back slammed the bricks and his dark eyes rounded with fear. "You're not going anywhere until you sing."

"I don't know nothing. We was just having some fun with you, is all."

"Fun?" Her adrenaline escalated again, only this time she was angry rather than scared. She guessed the guy who'd raped her had just been having fun, too. "Then how did you know I was a cop?"

He shrugged his thin shoulders.

Haven't you learned anything… The words of the warning note echoed through her head. *Another life's lesson for you.* Words so similar to those uttered by her rapist twelve years before. Not exactly the words of a street kid, either. Threatened sexual assault as an object lesson. Again.

Stella didn't believe in coincidences.

"What kind of a lesson were you supposed to teach me?" she asked.

"We was just supposed to scare you."

"On whose orders?"

The kid shook his head.

Did he not know or was he refusing to say?

Bluffing—he hadn't actually attacked her, so there was no point in arresting him—she said, "Maybe you want to tell your story to the judge."

Panic infused his slight body with strength that surprised her. He shoved her hard so she stumbled back, and as she swiped to grab him again, he ducked under her arm and ran.

"Stop!" she yelled.

The terrified kid ignored her and kept going. Stella's adrenaline pumped right out of her, and she let him go.

The last thing she needed was to run after trouble, and with no backup. Taking a careful look around to make sure no other dangers lurked nearby, she secured her gun and jogged to her car. Once in the front seat, she had to sit there until her hands stopped shaking.

She'd drawn her gun lots of times on the street, but she'd never shot anyone. She'd certainly never aimed it at anyone's head. At an unarmed kid's head. What else could she have done? What would they have done if she hadn't?

Nothing happened, she told herself. *So just calm down.*

Thankfully, she'd gotten away this time.

If they'd ever meant to hurt her at all.

THE CLUB WAS JUST OPENING when Gideon pressed a shoulder to the doorjamb, peered into the security office and watched his new security chief, who was intent on his work.

Gabriel Conner was the antithesis of John Logan in the appearance department. While Logan had worn designer suits and neatly spiked hair, Gabe lived in khakis and open-necked shirts, and his dark hair fell where it would without him apparently noticing. Gabe seemed more open than Logan while actually keeping more secrets. But then, Gideon had an edge there, having known Gabe before. In loyalty and work ethic, Logan and Gabe were equals, and that's all that really mattered to Gideon.

"Any luck?" he asked.

Starting, Gabe looked up from the computer. "Hey, Gideon. Depends on what you were hoping to find, I guess. Nothing but good on O'Rourke since he saw the light. Model citizen, working for the greater good. In addition to the counseling program he runs over in Humboldt Park, he's on the board of a city-wide non-profit organization that promotes mental health. Public works, private person. No flash, no dash, no hint of impropriety. The most shocking thing O'Rourke seems to have done is to quit the priesthood."

"A no-fault action. So what is it about him that's spooking Cass?" Gideon mused.

"She's still got her knickers in a twist, huh?"

"She says she sees something dark in his past, but she says it's something personal."

"Personal to whom? Stella or her?"

"Stella."

Though Cass had given up that information reluctantly. What had gone on between Stella Jacobek and Dermot O'Rourke in the past? he wondered. Could their situation simply remind Cass of something else? Someone else? A situation personal to *her*?

"Whatever Cass senses has me stumped," Gabe said. "I would bet my last dollar O'Rourke is a stand-up guy."

And if Gabriel Conner was anything, it was thorough, as Gideon knew firsthand under circumstances he would prefer to forget.

But that had been another life…

Lives…how many had he gone through now? Gideon wondered. More than Gabe had. More than he wanted to remember. He'd finally settled on one that seemed to make sense, at least in his skewed worldview.

"Good work," he told Gabe. "I don't suppose you got anything new on Tony Vargas."

Gabe leaned back in the office chair and, green eyes sparkling, laughed. "Only that he was a kick-ass fisherman."

"What?" Gideon grinned. "Trolling Lake Michigan for smelt?"

"No, really. A couple of years back, he won some kind of contest for the biggest walleye catch at Lake Geneva up in Wisconsin." Gabe tapped a few computer keys and said, "Take a look."

Gideon moved closer and peered over the other

man's shoulder at the LCD screen with its fuzzy photo of a scrawny, dark-haired young man standing on a pier in front of a fancy lake house. He was holding up his prize fish, basking under the admiration of a handful of onlookers on the patio behind him.

"Maybe it's not the same Tony Vargas. Not exactly an uncommon name."

"This Tony Vargas was from the south side of Chicago, however."

"Huh. Maybe it was him, then. What the hell would he be doing in Wisconsin? And where did a street kid learn to fish, anyway?"

"There's the lake...or what passes for a river practically outside their door," Gabe said.

Gideon could see it now—a bunch of tough Vipers hitting the streets, fishing poles in hand. Right. Not that it had any bearing on anything. The idea was so weird it simply aroused his curiosity.

"Print out a copy of that photo for the file on Vargas. O'Rourke or Stella can tell us if that's him for certain."

Before he finished, the printer was already spitting out the dead man's likeness.

Hours later, after being shown the computer-generated photo when he arrived at the club, O'Rourke agreed that this was *the* Tony Vargas.

"A fisherman," he mused, still staring at the print-out. "Now that's not something Tony ever talked about in our sessions. Maybe he lost his taste for all the waiting involved in getting a decent catch. Fishing is a patient man's sport and Tony was anything but patient." He tucked the photo back in the folder and handed it to Gideon. "So that's it?"

"That's all we've got. So far. Let's wait to see if Logan came up with anything new."

Not a long wait. Within the half hour, both Stella and Logan arrived and the whole crew filed into Gideon's office. As he settled behind his desk, Gideon noted how low-key Stella seemed tonight and wondered if she'd gotten some bad news or if she was simply discouraged.

His gazed fixed on her, he asked, "So who wants to go first?"

SINCE THE ATTACK Stella had been operating at low ebb. She couldn't even remember driving home. Suddenly she'd just been there and sweating over whether or not it was safe to go inside. Her own home!

Through a kind of haze, she listened to Gabe's discovery of Tony Vargas as an avid fisherman and to Logan's confirming that Norelli and Walker weren't looking elsewhere for a suspect and that they were especially pissed with *her* for hassling Luis Zamora.

"Louie Z.?" Blade asked.

Stella nodded. "Tip from Frank. Apparently, Luis plays poker with Johnny. And from what Señora Candera told me, there was some money issue between Luis and Tony."

"Blackmail," Gabe murmured.

"Maybe it was only poker. One way to find out— a visit to Skipper's."

Blade said, "Not you, not alone."

"Stella's not alone," Dermot countered. "She's with me now."

If she weren't feeling like the gum on the bottom of someone's shoe, his words might thrill her. As it was, Stella couldn't even decide exactly what Dermot meant by that statement.

He told the others about their convenient run-in with Alderman Marta Ortiz. "She was sure to remind us not to cross her."

"So I'll put the alderman at the top of my list," Gabe said. "If she's ever made a public wrong move, I'll find it."

"And I'll ask around Area 4," Logan added. "Just in case something got glossed over."

Stella realized everyone had been adding to the conversation except Cass. Standing a few yards away, her tight dress a shade of reddish purple that brought out the mahogany glint in her hair, she lounged against the wall, her attention focused directly on Stella, her expression worried and more intense than usual.

Giving Stella the weirdest feeling that Cass was rooting around in her mind.

What did she hope to find?

"Another thing," Dermot went on. "I had a conversation with the pastor of St. Peter's, and a couple of things he said got me thinking."

"About?" Gideon asked.

"About who might have real power, and not only now. Father Padilla is of the opinion that Johnny Rincon was only a figurehead leader of the Vipers."

"Johnny definitely had power," Blade argued. "His boys did whatever he told them."

"But what if someone was pulling *his* strings?" Dermot asked. "That speaks to Tony's complaints in our sessions—that someone had power over *him.*"

The suggestion finally engaged Stella. "You mean like a grand puppet master of the neighborhood?"

"Johnny," Blade said.

Dermot countered, "Or someone less likely."

"Huh." Stella looked to Logan. "Fingerprints?"

"Should have the results tomorrow."

Stella realized their shorthand had just gotten everyone's attention.

"Fingerprints on what?" Dermot asked.

"A note someone left last night at my door. A warning. 'Haven't you learned anything?'" she repeated from memory. "'Stay out of what isn't your concern and stay alive.'"

"Warning nothing. That's a threat! Why didn't you tell me about it?" Dermot demanded.

"I thought it might dim your enthusiasm for the hunt."

"Damn straight! I don't appreciate being kept in the dark, Star. If I had known—"

"What?" Stella asked, not liking the way Dermot had tensed and was now glaring at her. "What would you have done other than given me a hard time? I don't see how your knowing would've made any difference."

Stella blinked the other people in the room back into focus. She and Dermot might as well be alone for all the noise anyone else was making. Probably their argument startled the others into silence.

"What about the person who left the note?" Dermot asked. "Do you have any idea of who?"

"If I did, why would I need to run the fingerprints? Of course I never saw him."

"How could you have when he was playing Pin the Tail on the Donkey with me?"

Her turn to be shocked. "What!"

"I was barely on Halsted when I realized I was being followed. I lost them in Chinatown."

"Too bad you didn't get the license plate number," Gabe mused.

"I got part of it. XO 74 something."

"I'll have that run through the DMV database tomorrow," Logan said, "and see what I come up with. There can't be that many cars in this area that have plates built on those letters and numbers."

"Try a truck."

"Mmm, that'll narrow it down."

Stella couldn't believe Dermot's nerve. He was angry with her for not telling him about the note, but he was equally guilty at withholding information.

"Someone was playing bumper tag with you on the way home and you didn't fill me in when you saw me? Why not?"

"Because I just thought some kids were getting their jollies messing with me."

The breath caught in Stella's throat for a moment before she said, "Kids messing with you. Maybe. I didn't finish. The note isn't the end of it." Now she *had* to spill all. "On the way back to my car in Pilsen this afternoon, three street punks waylaid me."

Dermot's face reddened. "What!"

"Did they hurt you?" Gideon asked.

"No. I'm fine." Pulse accelerating at the memory, she quickly said, "The leader, Manny, threatened me, but I got the drop on the youngest one, and Manny and the other guy backed off. Weird thing is…I don't think they had weapons on them. It made me wonder if they'd have done anything to me, even if I hadn't gotten the drop on the kid.''

"What would be the point of the confrontation, then?''

Stella shrugged.

Dermot cut in, his voice tight. "You reported this and the note, right?''

"Neither. I wasn't hurt. No evidence of weapons. They would walk. As to the warning note, if I had turned it in for official investigation, I'd probably be ordered to cease and desist helping you for my own good.''

Dermot nodded. "You're out of this.''

Heat sizzled along Stella's nerves as it always did when she was holding on to her temper. "Oh, no. I'm not out of anything! I'm in it right up to my eyeballs. The puppet master theory works for me. The note and the message Manny relayed refer to the past. And the kid confirmed they were working on orders. I'm gonna find out who's behind this.''

Stella felt all eyes zero in on her, and she realized it had to do with her reference to the past. Only Dermot and Blade knew about the rape, and she wanted to keep it that way. The others didn't need details.

So all she said was, "A long time ago, I was thinking of revealing what I knew about a burglary, and a gang member tried to teach me a lesson then, too.''

Cass gasped. Stella had the uneasy notion that the other woman suspected what form the lesson had taken. Not that Stella would confirm it.

"Obviously, someone you or Dermot talked to has

spread the word that you're searching for the truth, and has put you in danger,'' Gideon mused.

"Johnny Rincon," Blade growled. "He's always hated Stella and me ever since I gave him that little present." He glanced at Dermot. "The scar he wears. My handiwork. He tried to threaten us into joining the Vipers."

"Maybe," Stella said, "but I still have doubts on that score. He left the Vipers behind years ago and went on to bigger crimes. Murdering Tony possibly among them. But the wording of the warnings...I don't know. Johnny tends to express himself more crudely."

"You really ought to stop, Stella," Cass suddenly said. "It's not safe for you. Lay low and let the rest of us take over."

Though her hair stood on end at the well-intentioned warning, Stella insisted, "I'm a cop." Whatever Cass *saw* couldn't stop her. "Nailing bad guys is my life. What kind of message would it send out if I lay low after being threatened? The word would spread faster than a speeding bullet. How could I do my job effectively after that?"

"If you don't survive you won't have the chance to do your job at all," Dermot growled.

"At least make yourself less available, away from the neighborhood," Cass suggested. "You can bunk in with me."

"Or me," Blade offered.

"I'm sure Lynn would appreciate that."

"She'd be glad to do it for someone else in trouble."

Reminded that the woman Blade loved and now

lived with had not only been her case, but had been the last victim to be helped by Team Undercover, Stella was actually considering the offer when Dermot said, "If anyone is going to play bodyguard, I will. It's my fault you got involved. This is all about me—"

"Not anymore, it isn't."

Stella knew she'd placed herself in the midst of a cat-and-mouse game, and suddenly she was one of the mice. No matter, she couldn't help but be irritated that everyone thought she needed to be protected. She was a cop and trained to protect herself, just as she'd done that afternoon.

Her practical side saw the wisdom of not being alone until the murderer was caught, however.

"All right. For the time being, I'll move in with Dermot," she agreed.

Her motivation was strictly case-related. A safety precaution. At the moment she wasn't feeling too kindly toward the man she'd vowed to exonerate.

Chapter Eight

The street that took them to Skipper's Tavern was lined with dollar stores, secondhand stores and a pawnshop. No fancy bookstores or coffee houses or sushi bars to tone up the neighborhood. According to Stella, the side-street corner establishment used to be the hotbed where everyone with a reputation or without a steady job gathered. At least that's what she was counting on.

His voice tight, Dermot asked, "You're sure you want to do this? Maybe we should give it a day."

"Maybe not."

Damn! Why had he agreed to let her drive?

They'd been on the way back to pick up his car and go to his place after Stella had packed what she needed for a few days, when she'd decided that now would be as good a time as any to check out Skipper's. Dermot wasn't fooled. Knowing he would object, she'd waited until they were almost there to tell him about their little detour.

"I never should have agreed to let you get me out of this jam," he muttered.

"Being the only suspect in a murder case is more

than a jam. And I didn't need your agreement. I simply thought things would go smoother if I had it."

"You don't owe me anything."

"So you keep saying."

Even if she hadn't believed him, Stella would undoubtedly do the same thing. That's the kind of cop she was. And the kind of person, he thought, as she slid the car to the curb.

Dermot was practically breathing down Stella's neck as she entered Skipper's—he wasn't about to let her get out of his reach. Once inside, she stopped suddenly and he bumped up behind her, making her gasp. Apparently still angry with him, she glanced back and frowned, then gave herself some space before looking around the smoke-filled room.

Dermot looked, too.

The guy behind the bar mixing drinks near the ship's wheel had to be the owner, Skipper. He wore a captain's cap and a cruise-ship-type shirt. The whole place was decorated to look like the inside of a ship. With a graying handlebar mustache and sideburns, Skipper was as hopelessly out-of-date as his nickname, but he perfectly fit his surroundings.

Dermot noted Stella had bypassed the pool table and dartboard areas to focus on the back of the room, where several guys played cards around a corner table. The only other woman present stood behind her man, whispering encouragement in his ear.

"Damn," she whispered. "No Johnny Rincon and no Luis Zamora. Illegal or not, those guys are playing for money. If Johnny *was* here, I'd be tempted to arrest him."

Personally, Dermot was glad the much-talked-about Johnny Rincon was absent tonight. Stella had been through enough in the past twenty-four hours. She didn't need to run up against a career criminal and possible murderer, as well.

"Why don't we leave, then," Dermot suggested, "and come back another time."

Maybe he could circumvent Stella altogether and get Blade to check out the joint the next day and see what he could dig up. Or there was that friend of his—Leroy. Maybe he'd already come up with something.

Stella ignored Dermot as if he hadn't spoken and stepped up to the bar. "Skipper. Long time."

"Well, aren't we honored to have one of Chicago's finest join us," Skipper announced loudly.

The tavern grew hushed, and Dermot noted all heads turned toward Stella. She slid onto a stool at the bar near the owner, and Dermot took the one next to hers. The guys at the poker table suddenly appeared nervous. Probably trying to decide what to do with a cop in the house. A cell phone flipped open and the player hit some number on his speed dial, then turned his back to the table, making Dermot wonder who he was calling.

Another man defiantly spread his cards across the table. "Read 'em and weep, boys."

But he didn't reach for the pot in the center until Stella turned her back on the rest of the room and concentrated on the bar owner.

"Two drafts. So how's business?"

Skipper grabbed two beer glasses and set them before the tap. "Same old, same old."

"All the usual suspects coming around?"

He laughed. "What is it you want, Detective?"

"Stella."

"And your friend is—"

"Not feeling very friendly tonight," Dermot muttered.

"Sorry," Stella said to Skipper.

"Don't apologize for me."

Skipper set their beers down before them. "Sometimes it doesn't pay to ask questions."

"Are you talking about yourself?" Dermot asked, handing the man a twenty. "Or about us?"

"I guess that depends on the question."

Stella beat Dermot to it. "Who are your regulars at the poker table?"

If anyone else in the room heard the question, he or she wasn't worried about the answer. Voices rose and mingled with the clack of cue tips against balls and the slap-slap of cards being dealt.

"I'm not running a casino here," Skipper was saying. "If the boys want to let off a little steam and pass a few bucks back and forth, that's their business."

"What boys?" Stella asked, then lowered her voice enough so no one but they could hear. "Johnny Rincon? Louie Z.?"

Dermot saw a clear *yes* reflected in Skipper's startled expression. But then he covered. "C'mon, you can't expect me to name names and stay in business."

"Louie Z...how often?" she continued to probe.

"Not often. And not anymore."

"Why? How big did he lose?"

Skipper spread his hands. "Since I have nothing to do with the game..."

"How often did Tony Vargas stop by?" Dermot asked.

Skipper winced. "Ah, the poor slob was here a lot. Said he had nothing better to do."

"Was he a player?"

"Look, I don't need no trouble here."

"Tony was murdered," Stella reminded him, taking over. And, as if she was officially investigating the case, she said, "If you withhold information…"

"Okay, so he was a player, so what?"

"Winner or loser?"

"Everyone knew Tony was a loser—"

"What about at poker?"

"Yeah, usually, but I hear he got lucky."

"How lucky?"

"I got another customer." Skipper escaped to the other end of the bar.

"Now what?" Dermot asked as Stella took another look around.

"Leroy."

He followed her gaze to the pool table. A slight man with thinning hair and a goatee hung up his cuestick and wandered over to where they sat.

"Stella, Blade says you're on the prowl for answers."

"That I am. How's the family?"

"Kids are eating me out of house and home," Leroy said, sounding like a proud dad. "Gotta pick up some extra work."

"Talk to Frank."

"Yeah, well…"

"Leroy's a mechanic," Stella said. "He used to work for my cousin Frank. Leroy…Dermot."

Leroy held out his hand for a shake. His strength for a small guy surprised Dermot. For some reason he'd sounded reluctant about approaching Stella's cousin—so maybe Frank had fired Leroy.

Stella said, "We were just asking Skipper about Tony's luck at the card table."

Leroy kept his voice low. "So-so, but he got lucky before he...well, you know."

"Right. Died. So did Tony score off anyone in particular?"

"Louie Z. lost to him big."

"How big?"

"Ten large."

Dermot whistled. "Ten thousand. I would swear he didn't collect. If Tony had his hands on ten grand, I would have known."

"Louie Z. didn't have it to give him." Leroy shook his head. "Tony scores the big one and what does he get for it? An IOU."

And maybe a rope around his neck instead? Dermot wondered. He glanced at Stella and was pretty sure she was thinking the same.

"How long ago was that?" she asked.

"Two weeks, give or take. Louie Z. hasn't been back since." Leroy glanced up and something like panic floated through his expression before disappearing. "Look, that's all I know," he said gruffly, backing away. "I can't tell you nothing else."

"You need something, Stella?" came a taunting voice from behind them. "You know I'm *the man*."

As Leroy beat a hasty retreat, Dermot whirled in his seat and came face-to-face with a pair of sleek designer sunglasses over a deeply scarred face. "You must be Johnny Rincon."

"My reputation has spread, huh?"

"Something like that."

"Reputation is very important to Johnny," Stella said in a way that sounded like a warning.

With his black leather jacket and slicked-back hair, Johnny Rincon looked like a cheap imitation of The Fonz in *Happy Days,* Dermot thought. Despite the low light in the room, the man didn't remove the sunglasses. He must like the effect. Probably thought not being able to see his eyes made him scary. That and the present from Blade.

Without taking his gaze from Dermot's, Johnny said, "You look familiar," and snapped his fingers at Skipper.

Knowing he was about five years older than Johnny—enough time for him to get out of town and in school before Johnny made his own reputation—Dermot said, "Mine was one of *the* faces of the neighborhood when you were just a snot-nosed kid."

Dermot felt Stella stiffen next to him, and he squeezed her knee to keep her from interfering. Before them, the man hardened and his mouth pulled into a thin line. Animosity pulsed from him in waves.

Suddenly the room narrowed to just the two of them—him and Johnny. Everything else—customers, Skipper, Stella—receded into the background. In a matter of seconds, twenty years of civilized behavior slid off Dermot like a snake's skin. Instinct swallowed him whole and spit out someone who could deal with a Johnny Rincon on his own terms, on his own turf.

"I wouldn't say that's very friendly," Johnny said, his voice low and threatening.

"He's not feeling very friendly tonight."

Dermot heard Skipper's edgy attempt at breaking the tension, but he kept the eye-lock with his target. "No disrespect intended."

"Johnny, on the other hand, disrespects everyone," Stella said. "Don't you, Johnny?"

"You need to watch yourself, Stella. Then, you always did have a problem with running off at the mouth. Don't you ever learn?"

Stella would have jumped at him if Dermot hadn't been faster. The second she squirmed, he snaked an arm around her waist and held her fast. He could feel her gun pressed against the inside of his arm, and he didn't want her to be obliged to pull it.

"Stay," he growled at her. To Johnny, he said, "Nothing like a woman with a big mouth and a bigger temper to make life interesting."

Johnny grunted but didn't let down his guard. "I know who you are." His lips turned into an imitation of a smile. "The holy-rolling shrink who hung Tony Vargas by his scrawny little neck." He shook his head. "What's the world coming to? Cops hassle an honest citizen like me, but they let a dangerous killer like you walk the streets."

Stella still clutched to his side, Dermot returned the feral grin. "I've never actually *killed* anyone…yet."

The tension was so thick in the room you could cut it with a knife. Not a sound intruded. Then Johnny barked a laugh and reached in between Dermot and Stella to the bar, where he fetched the glass and tall-necked bottle waiting for him. He tossed back the shot and washed it down with half a beer.

"Your boss know you're hanging with a criminal, Detective?"

"He has no idea I'm here with *you*, no. What about Louie Z., Johnny? Since when have you two gotten all cozy again?"

"Don't know who you've been talking to. It's just poker." He switched his attention back to Dermot. "Now that I think of it, I remember hearing how you put a guy in a coma."

"*He* survived."

"And after you spent time in juvy, you found religion."

"Which made me even tougher," Dermot told him. "But I *was* able to admit when I was outmaneuvered."

"Don't get too cocky." Johnny raised his beer in salute, then strolled toward the card game. "Or you might find you're not as tough as you think."

"WHAT THE HELL was all that macho posturing?" Stella demanded the moment they got in the car.

"I don't know what you mean."

"Liar." Not knowing when she'd ever been so irritated with Dermot, she started the engine and, with a jerk, wrestled the shift in gear. "What a performance."

"That was no performance," he assured her. "It was running on instinct. Self-preservation. The only thing someone like Johnny Rincon understands."

"For a minute there, you scared me."

"Remember who I used to be years before I met you."

"You're not that person anymore," she argued, trying to convince herself.

"Don't discount the past. We can never forget it completely. Yes, I've changed, but part of me will *always* be that tough gang kid I once was."

A fact that Stella had difficulty accepting, both for him and for herself.

She'd spent years fighting to stay out of a gang herself. She'd been raped when she'd threatened to cut a gang's criminal plans short. And she'd spent years as a beat cop helping to make gang members pay for their crimes.

So she didn't want to think about Dermot's early history. But apparently what she'd seen as a brilliant performance had been a slice of his own life.

She shuddered at the realization.

We can never forget it completely...

Not her, either. Did that make her a perpetual victim, someone always to be pitied? She hoped not.

Winding her way along a side street, she kept one eye on the rearview mirror for another set of lights that would indicate someone might be following them. To her relief, nothing. The street behind her remained free of another moving vehicle.

Dermot waited until they were on the main drag before asking, "So was tricking me into going to Skipper's worth the trouble? Was it good for you?"

She ignored his sarcasm. "We got three things confirmed. We know Officer Luis Zamora is associating with career criminal Johnny Rincon. Johnny knew about you being under suspicion for Tony Vargas's

murder, so that means Luis is probably the leak. And
we know Luis owed big money to Tony. We could
be dealing with a bad cop. I hope not. But it's not
looking good for Luis.''

''Too bad we didn't get anything new.''

''We did. Johnny's comment about my mouth, asking me if I ever learned…'' She shuddered again.

''You think he's connected to the threatening note
and the gang members who played you?''

''It's obvious that he knows about it. And the reference to the past…he knows about the attack, too.
Not that I'm surprised. He might not have been the
guy who raped me, but he was leader of the Vipers.
Undoubtedly he was the one who gave Rick Lamey
his orders to teach me that lesson.''

Stella didn't much feel like talking after that, and
thankfully neither did Dermot. Or perhaps he was
simply trying to be considerate. Whatever the reason,
they drove the rest of the way to the club in silence.

When he opened the door to trade cars, he asked,
''You're going to follow me, right?''

''That's the plan. Don't worry if you lose me. I
remember the address.''

''I'll wait for you outside the garage door.''

Having the short drive alone allowed her to cool
off. If they were going to be sharing a space for a
few days, tension was the last thing they needed between them. No matter what she told herself, however, Stella couldn't relax. Being alone with Dermot
in such close quarters was sure to be challenging.
Maybe staying miffed with him had its advantages.

Unfortunately, anxious was more where she was at.

By the time they got to his place in Printers Row

and left their cars in the small first-floor garage, Stella was having trouble breathing easily. When he insisted on carrying her bag and their hands collided as he got hold of the handle, her stomach tied in a knot.

Not an auspicious beginning.

Following Dermot from the garage onto the sidewalk and to the door, where he punched a code to get in, she asked, "What made you decide on the South Loop?"

"When I moved back to Chicago from D.C., a friend told me about this loft. The owner, a co-worker of my friend, had just gotten married and bought a house in a new development. He wanted to keep this place and rent it out, and I didn't see the downside. It's close to the lake and central to everything. The move couldn't have been easier."

Stella could see the draw of living in the conversion building in Printers Row, though she wasn't crazy about the rickety little elevator that took them to the fourth floor—the loft Dermot rented covered a good part of both that and the top floors.

Inside the loft, high ceilings, exposed brick walls and pegged plank floors all acknowledged the space's former use. The living and dining areas were part of a two-story atrium. They took circular metal steps that wound up to a half floor with a landing that circled the front of the loft. The side walls of the upstairs atrium area were lined with built-in bookcases that were more than half-full, while the front wall was all long windows, duplicating the lower half of the loft.

The main part of this floor was a bedroom.

One bedroom, Stella suddenly realized.

"There's an emergency exit to the hall on this

floor,'' Dermot said, indicating the door on the other side of the king-size bed. ''If you're in a hurry, you can use it to get to the elevator without going downstairs. And there's a service elevator in the other direction.''

''Just in case I found a really big clue and wanted to bring it up here?''

He barely cracked a smile at her attempted joke. ''Make yourself at home up here, Star. You can pretend I'm not even around.''

''Wait a minute. I'm not taking your bed from you.''

''Are you proposing we share it?''

Stella's pulse jumped, but of course he was kidding. ''I'm sleeping on the couch.''

''No way. The couch is mine.''

''Way. This is your place, I'm not gonna put you out.''

''You're not putting me out. You're letting me do what I want to do in my own home, and that's my couch.''

''And this is your bed.''

''Want to share?''

''Don't be ridiculous!''

Dermot's answering stare was steady and penetrating. ''Why ridiculous, Star?'' he asked softly, moving closer to her. ''I know you're as attracted to me as I am to you.''

Her heart banged against the wall of her chest at his words. He was attracted to her.

Or was it something else altogether, something that harked to the past? Was he mixing up the ongoing urge to protect her with attraction?

Until she could be sure...

Stella feared Dermot could hear the rush of her pulse as she said, "You offer me safe harbor so you can proposition me?"

"I just want my couch."

"All right, have the damn couch, then!"

"Thank you!" He grinned at her and stepped toward her.

"Don't be so smug or—"

"Or you'll what?" he asked, now so close she could hardly breathe.

What would she do? Stella wondered. She had no power over him. If anything, the reverse was true. The way his gaze was connecting with hers made her knees go weak, and she backed up against the atrium rail for support.

"Just...don't be so smug."

Dermot smiled, shook his head and started to step away. Then he stopped. Stared at her again. And moved so fast she didn't have time to react. Before Stella knew what was happening, he reached around her and grasped the rail behind her with both hands.

"What do you think you're doing?"

"Kissing you good-night. Unless you object."

"I—"

Not giving her time to protest, Dermot moved his mouth over hers. His lips were soft at first, then when she didn't try to free herself, they became more demanding.

Where was her strength when she needed it? Stella wondered as she failed to resist him.

She was a mass of contradiction, wishing to keep her distance, yet at the same time wanting him.

Raising her arms, she reached for him, surrounded his neck and pulled him closer. He let go of the railing behind her and encircled her waist so they were touching everywhere possible. Layers of clothing proved no barrier to desire. Her breasts ached, her belly tightened, her center heated and opened. All for him.

Being in Dermot's arms like this felt so right—could they have been meant to be together from the first?

Stella ignored the little voice inside her head telling her that in the morning she would regret any rash act. She wanted Dermot so much she couldn't resist the temptation of having him and thinking about it tomorrow.

Deepening the kiss, drawing his tongue more fully into her mouth, she rubbed her body none too subtly against his. Fire pulsed along her nerve endings, her breath quickened, and wet heat pooled along her thighs. When she felt his erection grow and press up against her belly, she tilted her hips so that she could trap his hardness and heat against her softness. He groaned and rocked against her, and Stella thought she might come apart without even undressing.

But no, that wouldn't be enough. She'd dreamed about this moment for so long.

More than anything, she wanted Dermot naked and pressing against her, flesh against flesh. She wanted to feel him touching her, stroking inside her, wanted to hear him whispering her name...

"Stella," he softly gasped, grasping her shoulders and setting her away from him, the gesture a rude awakening to her fantasy. His expression shocked, he murmured, ''That was some good-night kiss.''

With that, he brushed her forehead with his lips and left her standing there, staring after him in frustration, as he practically flew down the stairs and away from her.

Worse was the embarrassment that drew the heat from more tender parts up into her cheeks. Head clearing and aghast at her actions, Stella wished she could snap her fingers and disappear. She'd never felt so humiliated. How could she have pushed herself at a man who apparently didn't want her after all?

And how was she supposed to be comfortable with him now while they continued their search for the real killer?

Some people were too stubborn to learn from their mistakes, Stella Jacobek apparently being a prime example. Her private investigation into Tony Vargas's death continued.

Was it that she didn't understand the message?

Was it that she didn't care about the consequences?

Or was it that she thought—now that she was a hotshot detective—she was going to give a few lessons of her own?

Mistake after mistake after mistake…

Mistakes on both their parts. Trying to scare her simply had been a waste of time.

If she kept at it, sooner or later she was going to stumble on the truth…unless she was leaked more information meant to mislead her. Now, that might work. And if it didn't…well, if she were eliminated,

the dance still had a chance to be performed as cho-
reographed.

Sticking her nose where it didn't belong hadn't gotten Stella anything good the last time.

This time it might get her dead.

Chapter Nine

He'd had a hell of a night and the comfort level of the oversize couch had nothing to do with it.

Dermot gave up the ghost just before seven, put on a pot of coffee and jumped in the downstairs shower. Though he'd ended last evening in the same way— that shower cold—he'd tossed and turned throughout the night with little enough result. Always aware that Stella was but a winding staircase away, he'd slept in fits and starts. He seemed to have been tuned in to her every sigh, her every movement. He'd known when she'd rearranged the pillows and when she'd gotten up in the middle of the night to stand at the railing and stare down at him.

As long as Stella was staying at his place, Dermot doubted he would get much sleep.

When she'd pushed him away the first time they'd kissed, he'd figured she still wasn't comfortable with her own sexuality. But considering what had almost happened between them the night before, it seemed he wasn't giving her enough credit. And truth be told, he was thankful he'd had enough sense to stop things before they'd gone any further. He couldn't do that to her—making love to her without telling her the whole truth would be another betrayal.

The seal of the confessional was a heavier burden now than ever.

As he toweled himself dry, Dermot heard the upstairs shower start and an immediate image of Stella soapy and naked and too inviting came to him. His reaction was instantaneous. Cursing, he hit the cold water handle and stepped back under the needle-fine spray for another rude awakening.

By the time Stella came downstairs, he was thankfully in control of himself, fully dressed and in the midst of scrambling eggs in the kitchen area that was open to the rest of the loft. He hadn't done much with the place. He'd moved in his furniture—basic black-and-gray guy stuff—and that was it. Dressed in a red boatneck sweater and pants, her golden brown hair spilling over both shoulders, Stella added a flash of warm, inviting color to an otherwise dreary indoor landscape.

"Coffee?" Dermot asked, trying to sound normal.

"Please."

He filled a mug and pushed it toward her over the granite countertop. "Do you like cheese in your eggs?"

"I'm not really hungry."

"But you're eating."

"Sounds fine."

Great, Stella was acting weird around him now. That wouldn't do. He grabbed dishes and flatware and pushed them toward her.

"Could you set up the table?"

Nodding, she did as he asked without comment.

After pouring the eggs into the frying pan, he pulled a carton of berry punch and a bowl of strawberries from the fridge and handed her those. He noticed how her hand jumped away from his so she wouldn't touch him.

"About last night—"

"Let's not."

"Star, don't shut me out, please. I was inappropriate and I apologize."

"You?"

"Yes, me. I never should have kissed you, but you were simply irresistible."

"It didn't seem that way to me."

"It was the whole couch-bed argument. I simply got carried away. But that wasn't fair. I brought you here to protect you, not to take advantage of you."

"Excuse me, but no one takes advantage of me. I have my own mind."

"I'm very aware of that."

"And I don't need protection."

"If you say so."

"Oh, don't start."

That was it, he had her arguing. "Would you feel better if I let you throw me so you could prove how big and strong you are?"

"Is this straight out of Psych 101 or what?"

"How about Smile, Why Don't You? at whatever level you choose?"

Apparently Stella couldn't help herself, because her mouth softened at the title of his made-up course, and a second later she was grinning. The wide smile lit her whole face. Once more struck by her warmth and beauty, Dermot had to fight his own physical reaction and keep things light between them.

"That's better," he said.

"Is it? Your eggs are burning."

"Go ahead and laugh." He pretended insult. "You're going to have to eat them."

At least Stella did so with better humor than she'd started the morning, which relieved Dermot. They couldn't very well work together with negative tension between them. At least they couldn't do so effectively.

They kept up the banter through breakfast.

Afterward, cleaning up with Stella's help—bringing her a little too close for his comfort—Dermot forced himself to focus on Tony's murder.

"Now what?" he asked. "Do you have a plan for the day?"

"I'm out of ideas until I get something to go on," Stella admitted as she set coffee mugs in the dishwasher. "I thought I would call home and see if I have any messages. I was hoping Logan ran those plates. And maybe got an ID off the fingerprints. My cell phone's upstairs."

"The house phone is on the counter."

She called while he cleared and wiped down the counter and stove. For a moment she seemed very intense. He didn't say a word, though, lest he make her miss something.

Hanging up, she turned to him, her expression thoughtful.

"Logan?" he asked.

She nodded. "And Frank. Logan learned the license plates are registered to a man named Hector

Santos. He lives a couple of blocks down from the museum. The fingerprint belongs to one Manuel Santos at the same address.''

''Looks like Manny has been a busy boy. Leaving you the threat, tailing me, waylaying you to scare you.''

Stella sighed. ''Now if only we can find out who gives him his marching orders…''

''So let's pay the Santos household a visit.''

''Exactly what I had in mind. After which, it'll be time for fiesta.''

''You want to party?'' Dermot asked.

''Frank gave me another heads-up. Word is Marta Ortiz plans to eulogize her dear departed cousin Tony at the opening of the Day of the Dead festivities.''

''You think she'll have something good to say about Tony?''

''She's a politician and he was her cousin. What do you think?''

''I think it should be interesting to see how she makes a small-time criminal sound like a saint.''

THE SANTOS APARTMENT took up the front half of its building's second floor and perched over an old-fashioned tavern on the corner. A couple of shrieking kids came running down the stairs as Stella tried to make her way up with Dermot following. A short, gently rounded woman in a flowered dress stood on the second-floor landing and yelled down at them in Spanish to stay off the street.

Stella figured she was wasting her breath. The streets around here were the neighborhood playgrounds, and kids rarely listened to grown-up warnings, anyway.

The woman was about to go back into her apartment—so hoping she spoke English, Stella called, "Mrs. Santos?"

"Yes?"

Only a hint of an accent. Good. That made things easier.

"Detective Stella Jacobek." She pulled out and opened her identification, then held it up so the woman could see it as she and Dermot caught up to her. "I need to talk to you."

Mrs. Santos mumbled something under her breath and crossed herself. Her dark eyes were panicky as she asked, "Is someone dead?"

Stella's stomach knotted at the question. What must it be like to live on a daily basis in fear of your loved ones dying, no doubt because of the gang wars? This woman appeared to be young—maybe in her mid-thirties or so—too young to consider losing a child or husband.

"No one in your family," Stella assured her. At least not that she knew, Manny being a wild card and all. "But I need to ask you some questions about a coupla things that happened in the past few days. Can we come in?"

Glancing from Stella to Dermot, Mrs. Santos nodded.

They followed her into an apartment that was both shabby yet inviting. The furniture and rugs were old but clean, and except for a few toys strewn across the living room floor the place was in order. The walls were a bright turquoise and dotted with religious artifacts and family photos. And small vases of flowers were set in areas where the smaller kids couldn't knock them over.

Twisting her hands together, Mrs. Santos asked, "What is it you want with me?"

"Hector Santos," Dermot said. "Is he your husband?"

"Yes, but he's not here now. He's at work," she gasped, "isn't he?"

"Probably," Dermot murmured reassuringly. "As far as we know."

"What about Manny?" Stella asked.

"My oldest son."

"Is he home?"

Mrs. Santos shook her head. "What has he done now?"

The woman's expression grew even more frightened, convincing Stella she knew about his gang involvement. She hated giving the poor woman the bad news.

"He and two other boys stopped me in the street and threatened me yesterday."

"No!" Mrs. Santos whispered, her attempt at denial weak. She mumbled a quick prayer to the Lord in Spanish.

"I'm afraid he did, Mrs. Santos, though he didn't actually hurt me. I also believe Manny delivered a threatening message to my home."

Dermot added, "And we think he used your husband's truck to follow me the other night."

Even as she said, "No, not my Manny," belief mixed with fear for her son in her eyes.

Knowing she wasn't really disillusioning the other

woman, Stella asked, "How long has Manny been a Viper?"

Manny's mother began to shake. Dermot gently patted her shoulder.

"Perhaps you would like to sit?"

Mrs. Santos nodded and sank to the couch. So that she could be at eye level with her, Stella took the chair opposite, while Dermot continued to stand behind her, placing a hand on her shoulder in support. Affected as always by his touch, she glanced up at him and caught his compassionate expression for the distraught woman.

"I told him to leave the gang alone," she began, "but he wouldn't listen to me or his father. They get them so young, before you even know it. Manny used to go out of his window at night and climb down the drainpipe. He doesn't bother hiding what he's doing anymore." She gave Stella an imploring look. "Isn't there anything we can do so you don't have to put my Manny behind bars?"

"I'm not here to arrest him."

The woman looked at her as though she didn't understand. "But you said he did these bad things…"

But not bad enough or with proof enough to make an arrest stick, and Stella knew it. Taking him in would only generate paperwork, and in the end, he would probably walk.

"Well, he didn't hurt either one of us this time," she said. "And someone put him and the others up to no good. *That's* the person I want."

"Others?" Mrs. Santos echoed. "Which boys?"

"I didn't get one of the names. The youngest was called Pablo."

When Mrs. Santos dropped her face in her hands and began sobbing, Stella knew she'd been right. She glanced back at Dermot and mouthed the words *Manny's brother.*

Dermot walked over to the couch and sat beside the woman. "I know this is very difficult for you," he said, "but your boys don't have to turn out bad. If you can't get them out of the neighborhood, then ask for help to get them out of the gang."

"Who would help us? Not the police."

"Father Padilla at St. Peter's. He helped *me* find a different path almost twenty years ago. He's still trying to stop the gang wars."

Eyes wet, Manny's mother gazed at Dermot with a mixture of puzzlement and hope. "*You* were a Viper?"

"An Eagle. Just as tough."

Stella knew the gang called themselves Eagles because in the wild, eagles killed snakes. And in the neighborhood, Eagles sometimes killed Vipers. If she hadn't seen his transformation for herself the night before at Skipper's, Stella would be hard-pressed to believe Dermot had been one of them.

She said, "A good start would be by weakening the Vipers themselves. Someone has a hold on the gang, and if we only knew *who*—"

"But I don't know!" Mrs. Santos cried.

"Has Manny ever mentioned anyone asking him to do things…favors, perhaps?" Dermot asked.

The woman's face darkened. "Some guy named Paz. Paz Falco."

"I don't know him," Stella murmured. "Though the name is familiar. Then again, I've been away from this district for a while now. Not to say I ever knew everyone's names anyway.''

"Or he could be new to the neighborhood,'' Dermot suggested.

"Maybe,'' Mrs. Santos said, but she didn't sound certain.

"Is Paz the only one who had influence over Manny?'' Stella asked. "No one else?''

The woman thought hard for a moment. "A few days ago, he got a call from someone I didn't know. The minute he put that phone down, he headed for the door. I asked him to watch the little ones for me while I went to the store. He said he didn't have time, that he had something more important to do.''

"When was that exactly?''

"Day before yesterday.''

The same day she'd gotten the written warning and Dermot had been followed. "You took the call?''

"Yes.''

"Can you remember anything about the caller's voice or what exactly was said? Did the person speak English or Spanish?''

"She was speaking Spanish, and she just asked for Manny. That's all.''

Stella's pulse fluttered. "*She?* The caller was a woman? Or was she younger? Another teenager?''

"Maybe.''

But she didn't sound convinced of that, either.

Stella spent a few more minutes trying to get information from her, but the woman didn't have any more to give. Stella indicated to Dermot that they should go. He nodded, then reminded Mrs. Santos about contacting Father Padilla for help with her sons.

She smiled and murmured, *"Gracias,"* before turning to Stella. "I am so sorry for whatever my sons thought they would do to you. I will tell my husband, and together we will have words with both Manny and Pablo when they get home." She shook her head. "Threatening a woman…"

Hoping the woman understood the nature of the threat and would truly do something to show them the error of their judgment, Stella smiled and wished her luck before leaving the apartment.

Out on the street, she said, "So some mystery woman snapped her fingers and Manny jumped."

"Now all we have to do is get a name."

"We only have one woman suspect in Tony's murder," Stella reminded him.

Alderman Marta Ortiz.

STELLA FOLLOWING close behind, Dermot fought the crowd that surged around the Mexican Fine Arts Center Museum as Los Dias De Los Muertos got underway. It was the day before Halloween, and the Pilsen fiesta would run four afternoons and evenings, combining the Anglo and Mexican celebrations. The street in front of the museum entrance had been barricaded, cutting off all but pedestrian traffic—residents and tourists alike.

Dermot stopped at a vendor cart and bought two walnut-size *calaveras*—sugar skulls decorated with colored icing and candy beads, which were given to friends like Valentines. He handed one to her.

"Souvenir?" She admired the workmanship before slipping it into her jacket pocket.

"Appropriate for the occasion, don't you think?" Dermot asked, popping his into his mouth.

Other vendors sold skeletons, skull masks and other macabre toys; *papel picado*—intricate tissue paper cutouts; fancy wreaths and crosses decorated with silk flowers; candles and votive lights; and *pan de muertos,* a bread baked in the shape of a skeleton, person or animal, which represented the souls of the dead. Along with photos, candles, crosses and flowers, the bread might be set on an *offerenda* or altar such as the one that flanked one side of the museum grounds. The soul of the bread was to be consumed by the dead when they visited, and what was left was then consumed by the living.

Many who didn't understand the tradition found eating food in the shape of skulls and skeletons morbid, Stella knew, but the intention was that by eating them you were looking at yourself as a dead person and, in a humorous way, cheating death itself.

"There's the alderman," Stella said, stopping and pointing to Marta Ortiz, who held court over several well-dressed people just to the side of the *offerenda.*

Dermot pulled Stella closer, close enough to smell the subtle fragrance of spice in her hair that distracted him from coherent thought. That made him want to take her in his arms and never let her go.

Then he pulled himself together. "Do you recognize her admirers?" he asked softly, bending slightly so his lips were close to her ear.

Stella turned her head so quickly, their lips almost brushed. Dermot caught his breath and waited for her reaction as their gazes connected. A flicker in her eyes told him what he wanted to know. She licked her lips, and he swore he could smell musk blended with the spice. Gut knotted with wanting her, he nevertheless backed off.

Stella blinked, took a big breath and returned her attention to Marta Ortiz and companions. "Another alderman," she said, sounding a bit breathless. "A state representative. A museum board member or two."

"She certainly has clout."

"So she warned us. Why would she feel it necessary if she wasn't trying to hide something?"

"Why, indeed?"

Since the festivities were traditionally late in getting started—today seemed to be no exception—Dermot escorted Stella through the crowd and into the museum to take a quick pass at the largest Day of the Dead exhibit in the nation. He was careful to stay close without actually touching her despite the number of people crammed into such a small space.

"Death is such a serious topic. I wonder how it started—combining the seriousness of a holy day with humor and the joy of remembering loved ones."

Stella was examining a display of folk art, which provided a colorful and sometimes mirthful interpretation of death. Some of the people around them wore pins or earrings or even masks that played on the death theme. One guy dressed all in black and wearing a skeleton face was pretty spooky, and Dermot wondered if he weren't testing his Halloween costume.

"Probably they picked up on the Aztec view of death as part of the eternal cycle rather than as an end," Dermot said. "Not all that different from the

Christian belief in heaven. I guess that's why the official Day of the Dead is the same as the Catholic All Souls' Day on the first of November when we pray for those suffering in purgatory.''

To his surprise Dermot found himself saying a quick prayer for Tony Vargas. The ex-con had been a lot of things, but he hadn't been violent.

''Maybe we should get back outside,'' Stella said, starting to sound impatient. ''We don't want to miss anything.''

''Right.''

Dermot followed while still thinking of the man who was about to be eulogized. In his own bizarre way, Tony had tried to stop the planned attack on Stella. But no matter his personal philosophy, he'd died violently himself. And while Dermot hoped to clear his own name, he also wanted to find Tony's murderer before someone else was killed.

Would the killer be in the crowd outside the museum?

Chapter Ten

What Stella couldn't miss when they found a spot within view of the altar was Marta Ortiz conferring with Luis Zamora. They stood off to one side of the museum, heads together.

"Louie Z.," she murmured.

"Significance?" Dermot asked.

She shrugged. "I'm not sure. It's natural that they would know each other since Luis patrols this part of her ward. Maybe he's helping provide security."

But even as she said the words, they rang false for Stella. There was something…well, odd…about the way the cop and the alderman huddled close, expressions serious as if they were plotting together.

Tony was Marta's cousin…Luis owed Tony money…Luis might or might not be involved with Johnny Rincon. Now, if she found anything to connect Johnny back to Marta…what then?

Stella simply didn't know.

"Do you see what I see?" Dermot asked as Marta broke from Luis and headed for the altar and podium.

Detectives Norelli and Walker were standing off to one side. Stella figured they'd heard about the alderman's intended eulogy and were scanning the assemblage to see who showed, just as she and Dermot were doing. But why? They'd nabbed their suspect—*Dermot*—and certainly hadn't seemed interested in moving on to anyone new.

"Yep," she said. "And they see us."

Both detectives were staring their way now. With no guilt over helping an innocent man, Stella stared back. She sensed Dermot doing the same. And why shouldn't he? He had no reason to feel guilty about anything. No reason at all.

Norelli was the first to look away, and within seconds so did Walker. Both detectives drifted into the throng, past a couple of kids wearing skull masks who were strewing marigold petals along the sidewalk in front of the museum. The bright yellow paths were meant to create a bridge between the worlds of the living and the dead.

But Stella wasn't paying strict attention to the ceremony's start, introduced by some museum board members. Instead, she scanned the assemblage, dozens of people deep in every direction, her thoughts following the detectives and their purpose here today.

Had they simply wanted to see if Dermot would show up for Tony's eulogy?

What would that prove?

Suddenly she became aware of Vipers in the crowd—small knots of them. Eagles to the west. Latin Kings to the east. Vipers to the south. She wondered if Manny was one of the tough-looking teenagers hiding his identity behind a skull mask. The thought made her uneasy, made her wonder what his purpose here was today. Could he be looking for her, meaning to finish what he'd started? If so, he had enough re-inforcements to do the job.

Shuddering, she was about to point out the gang members to Dermot, when Marta Ortiz stepped up to the mike.

"Violence as a way of life, as a solution to our problems, is never acceptable," she began. "Tony Vargas died violently last week, and I am here before you today to mourn my younger cousin."

The alderman was at her best—her voice husky with grief, yet strong with anger. The sincere politician appealing to the masses. As Marta went on, painting a portrait of a Tony that Stella had never met, Stella looked around and tried to figure whether or not everyone bought it.

"Tony was not perfect, certainly," Marta was saying, "but I remember him as a kid who tried to please everyone...until the Vipers got hold of him. Then he changed before my eyes into someone only out for himself. Protect your children!" she implored, her gaze meeting those of individual after individual. "And fight the gangs to extinction!"

A murmur went through the throng, and Stella looked back to where present-day Vipers congregated. One of them sent a rude gesture the alderman's way, but the others simply seemed to be amused. Or bored.

"I don't see Manny," she told Dermot, "but I would bet he's here, hiding behind one of those masks. Maybe Pablo is with him, too."

"If you do spot them, tell me. After what they did to you, I'd like to have a private chat with them myself."

A thrill shot through Stella. And a sense of dismay. While touched that Dermot still wanted to be her champion, she wasn't a victim anymore. He didn't have to fight her battles for her. Until he understood that…

"Don't start any trouble," was all she said.

"Me? Three gangs showed," Dermot observed. "Now *that* has the makings of trouble."

"I sincerely hope not. Too many innocent bystanders could get hurt."

Stella scanned their faces—worried parents, concerned businessmen, indifferent teenagers. Her gaze lit on a pair of designer sunglasses, and the noise of the speech and the crowd's reaction faded fast.

Johnny Rincon was there, in the thick of things, his interested gaze not on Marta but on Stella herself. Why the interest? Simply because she'd shown up at Skipper's the night before and asked too many questions? Did that mean he had something to hide? Continued gang activity? Burglaries? Murder?

Johnny smiled at her, the scar splitting one side of his face, a macabre reminder of the kind of human being he wasn't. He didn't need a mask to fit in—he looked like walking death to Stella. He saluted her…then turned away to be swallowed by the masses.

Heart thundering, Stella tuned back in to the alderman's performance.

"Tony isn't the only one I mourn today," Marta Ortiz was saying. "My younger brother was a tragic victim, as well. Two members of my family lost to gangs and violence! I say…*enough!*"

The crowd roared to life with applause as Stella

admitted Marta Ortiz's words sounded more like a campaign speech than a remembrance of a lost loved one. But even so, she had said something telling.

Lost.

Lost to gangs and violence.

Rather than looking to Dermot to accuse him of murder—to Stella's complete surprise—the alderman had pinned the blame elsewhere. Why? Could it be that, without being the actual villain of the piece, Marta knew more about her cousin's death than she'd let on?

The more facts and suppositions Stella gathered, the more overwhelmed she felt by the responsibility of reading things right.

The crowd quieted and the alderman concluded her speech. But even before the applause died down, Stella overheard a couple of young men's comments.

"She might have good intentions for her people, but she's got better ones for herself," one guy said.

He and his friend looked kind of artsy—artists seeking cheap studio rentals being the newest element in the neighborhood mix.

"I hear she wants to run for state office next," said the friend.

"She'd better have deep pockets."

"Or rich friends. I've heard she's none too fussy about how she lines her campaign coffers."

The men laughed and moved on.

The crowd in front of the museum broke up into small groups of families and friends intent on having a good time. Strolling mariachis lured a large group of laughing people to park grounds, thinning the num-

ber of warm bodies in front of the museum to something less than smothering.

"Let's check out the messages on the board,"
Stella suggested.

She indicated the big corkboard that was set to one
side of the *offerenda*. There, audience members could
leave photographs or written thoughts about whatever
dearly departed person they were celebrating. Stella
started to check the missives at one end, Dermot at
the other. It didn't take her long to find what she was
looking for.

"Yep, here's one about Tony."

Dermot drew closer so they were shoulder to shoulder before the board. For a moment she could hardly
breathe. Touching him was too, too distracting. It
took all her will to focus on the messages.

"'Tony, you were a great guy,'" she read.
"'We're gonna miss ya.' Sounds like a high school
yearbook entry."

"How about this one," Dermot said. "'You didn't
deserve to die so young. You shoulda had that second
chance.'"

Stella read several more in the same vein. In death,
his many sins forgiven, Tony Vargas was almost re-
vered. Unfortunately, that wasn't exactly helpful to
the case.

"Whoa," Dermot muttered. "We might have
something here. 'Tony died as secretively as he lived.
Look to the last person you would suspect to find his
killer.'"

"Marta Ortiz?" Stella asked softly. "That'd fit.
And it'd be fitting, considering she just gave a campaign speech disguised as a eulogy."

"But more than that—" Dermot's forehead pulled into a frown "—it's almost as if someone was talking straight to us, trying to give us a clue."

"But not one that's very clear." Stella took the sheet from the board by its edge, carefully trying not to smudge it, folded it and slipped it into a pants pocket. "Fingerprints," she said. "If I can get an ID on whoever wrote this, maybe we can get him or her to spill the rest. I'll pass this on to Logan tonight. If we're lucky, we could have a name tomorrow."

"Even if you do pin down the author, do you really think he or she would come clean?"

She shrugged. "It's worth a shot."

The area around the museum was quickly revving up into party mode. Not much more they could do here, so they bought plates of assorted Mexican food from one of the vendors and were able to get a spot at one of the temporary picnic tables set up in the barricaded street. Stella had barely bitten into her steak taco before feeling the hairs on the back of her neck bristle. She caught movement from the corner of her eye and swiveled on her bench just in time to see a figure in black wearing a skull mask turn and walk away.

Still, her flesh crawled.

"Something wrong?" Dermot asked.

"I got the feeling I was being watched," Stella told him. But when she glanced back again, the figure was gone. "My imagination, I guess."

At least, that's what she told herself.

As they ate, they went over the details of what they knew yet again. But Stella was left with no new ideas of how to proceed.

Not wanting Dermot to lose hope, she smiled and prayed she wasn't lying when she said, "Something will break soon. We just have to keep chipping away."

Once they finished their meals, with nothing left to accomplish in the neighborhood, they decided to go back to Dermot's place for showers and a change of clothing before heading for the club. Knowing how crowded it would be around the museum, they'd left the car parked in front of the Santos' apartment, which was a few blocks south.

Stella was enjoying the fine autumn weather and the relaxed stroll with Dermot until they got within sight of his vehicle. Detectives Mike Norelli and Jamal Walker had beaten them there and were leaning on the car.

Dermot cursed under his breath and said, "This can't be good."

While Stella agreed, she didn't say anything until they were within yards of the two men. Norelli's smug expression put her more on edge. And Walker was outright grinning at them as if he was the cat who'd swallowed the canary.

"Detectives," she said, her voice stiff.

"What now?" Dermot asked, unable to hide his exasperation.

Norelli waved a paper in front of his nose. "It's called a search warrant."

Dermot grabbed it, looked it over and passed it to Stella, asking, "What haven't you searched?"

"Your vehicle," Walker said. "So unlock the doors and open the trunk."

A quick glance at the paperwork told Stella everything was in order. Dermot beeped open the car doors, and Norelli started with the glove compartment, while Walker slid a hand under the driver's seat.

"Guys, what's going on here?" Stella asked. She had a really bad feeling about this.

"We're doing our job nailing a murderer," Norelli informed her, closing the glove compartment and sticking a hand under the passenger seat.

"You have the wrong man."

Walker grinned harder. "So *you* say."

"Just open the damn trunk!" Norelli groused.

Knowing there was more going on here than they'd admitted, Stella felt her stomach knot. "Why the car, why now?"

"We got a tip, okay?"

"Who tipped you?" Dermot asked as he unlocked the trunk.

"A reliable source," Walker said.

Which meant some scumbag off the streets who could be bought, Stella thought. She didn't know what they expected to find inside the trunk—a body, perhaps? As the trunk lid slid open, she caught her breath…then let it out in relief when nothing obvious jumped out at them.

Norelli cursed and Walker practically climbed into the trunk to search it. He pulled and pushed at every item, until at last a sound of triumph escaped him.

"What?" Stella demanded.

Walker's dark face was split in a grin as he turned, the object he'd been searching for in his hand. "Dermot O'Rourke, you're under arrest for the murder of Tony Vargas. Norelli, read him his rights."

Stella noted Dermot looked as dumbstruck as she felt.

From Walker's hand hung a purple velvet rope.

"SOMEONE SET DERMOT UP," Stella said several hours later, as she finished telling the members of Team Undercover what had happened.

Gathered in Gideon's office, the others sat while Stella paced, as if she could work off the stress that threatened to consume her. She'd already given the note from the message board to Logan, who'd promised to ask the lab to run fingerprints first thing in the morning.

"How in the heck did someone plant the velvet rope in Dermot's trunk without his knowing?" Cass asked. "I mean, it's a new car with an antitheft system, right?"

"That doesn't matter," Logan said. "An experienced car thief can get into any vehicle."

"And there's been auto theft and chop shop operations in that area since we were kids," Blade added. "While we were working on Lynn's case, guess who offered to get me the car of my dreams…cheap."

"Not Johnny," Stella said.

"Yes, Johnny."

"But I don't understand how Dermot could have missed a purple velvet rope in his trunk," Cass said. "Unless it happened earlier today during the Day of the Dead festivities. Of course, that was broad daylight with thousands of people around."

"Not necessarily," Stella said. "It could have been planted the other night, when Dermot was followed.

Or the night Tony died, for that matter. Maybe even while Dermot was still working in Heartland House.''

Gideon arched his eyebrows. ''Now, that would have been a bold move.''

''What do you call murdering Tony where his roommate could walk in at any moment?''

Stella hadn't taken an easy breath since the arrest. She'd gone over every possible scenario in her mind. Not that it was doing Dermot any good. *She* wasn't doing Dermot any good. She'd failed him miserably.

Blade asked, ''You called Stark?''

Thinking of the criminal lawyer, she nodded. ''I gotta thank Lynn again for hooking Dermot up with Stark. He said he'd get on it right away. Now I just gotta figure out how to find the money to bail Dermot out. Assuming the judge sets bail, this being a murder case.''

She thought Dermot would get bail, but you never knew. And while the victim had been a criminal himself, he'd also been related to someone with clout.

''Stark will convince the judge,'' Blade assured her.

''And I've got the bail money,'' Gideon added.

Stella gasped. ''What?'' The generous offer left her speechless.

Gideon waved his hand as if it were nothing. ''It's only ten percent of whatever the judge sets.''

''We're talking about murder. Ten per cent could be a hundred grand.''

''I know that.''

''Gideon, I can't ask you—''

''You haven't. I volunteered.''

''Thank you.'' Tears stung Stella's eyes at his generosity. They were all generous, giving of their time to someone they didn't even know. "I'll owe you, all of you, I really will."

"You already owe me," Gideon said, smiling, "so what's a little money? Not that I'm counting. I'm going to do this because I want to. It's probably too late in the day for an arraignment. Undoubtedly Dermot will have to wait until morning to get sprung."

"Which means he'll be stuck at Area 4 for the night."

The idea of Dermot spending even a single night behind bars crushed Stella. Her fault. Her failure. He was innocent—why couldn't everyone see that?—and she hadn't been able to find the real murderer. What kind of detective did that make her? she wondered, as Gideon picked up the phone and hit a number on his speed dial.

Of course not everyone knew Dermot the way she did. *Not everyone loved him.* Stella's heart pounded at the thought she'd been trying to put to the back of her mind while she worked with the man to clear him.

"Stark? Gideon here."

Stella stopped to listen, but apparently Gideon was talking to Stark's voice mail. As he left a message about the bail money, Stella's thoughts drifted back to Dermot and how much she still loved him. Or perhaps how she really loved him for the first time.

Twelve years ago, she hadn't known the real Dermot O'Rourke. She'd heard about his troubled past, but she hadn't seen that side of his personality. Now she had—she knew everything there was to know about him and it didn't make any difference to her. She loved Dermot for who he was at the time he'd saved her. For who he had been before that. For the decisions he'd made in his life that had led him to where he was now. For the person he'd become.

"No luck in catching Stark," Gideon said, setting the cell phone down on his desk.

Gabe added, "You might as well go home and get a few Zs."

"Yeah, maybe that's best," she agreed.

If she could sleep. And whose home? Hers or Dermot's? He'd given her a set of keys, so she had her choice.

"I'll walk you out," Cass said.

Stella waited until they'd gotten away from the office door and down the hall before stopping. "Okay, what's on your mind?"

Cass shook her head. "It's what's on yours."

"I got a lot on mine."

"He'll get through it. I've been there. Not that there was anyone to help *me*," Cass said bitterly. "Not even Max Street."

"Max Street?" Stella echoed. "As in Maxwell Street, the magician?"

Cass nodded. "My boss and...friend. At least I thought he was."

Stella had a gut feeling that Max had been more to Cass than boss and friend. From the fleeting pain she glimpsed in the other woman's expression, the connection had gone way deeper.

Before Stella could tactfully figure a way to ask, Cass said, "We won't let Dermot go to prison for something he didn't do."

"I'm sorry it happened to you, Cass."

"Yeah, well…it's in the past. I survived, and I guess that's what matters."

But Cass had been incarcerated for jewel theft, not murder. Two years wasn't the same as potentially being sentenced to life. Or death.

Stella wanted to believe that Cass was right, that her gift allowed her to see Dermot free, his name cleared. But she knew it didn't work that way. Cass merely got impressions—and was a pretty positive person most of the time—while all Stella had to go on was faith and her own determination.

They turned the corner and walked toward the stairs jammed with people waiting to get seated in the club. Music blasted them from the open doorway of the lower entrance. Stella was about to say her goodbyes when she stopped short and backed up away from the stairs and around the corner, pulling Cass with her.

"What?" Cass asked, her voice low.

"The woman in red two steps up?" Stella said, indicating Cass should take a peek. "That's Alderman Marta Ortiz." Red, a real expression of mourning, Stella thought. Maybe for gypsies, but not for a Latina… "And her escort is one of the politicians who was at the Day of the Dead festivities."

"How interesting," Cass said, her grin wide.

"What are you thinking?"

"That Mags looks like she could use some help with her hostess duties. Stay put, out of sight, and I'll be back in a few minutes."

Glancing around the corner, Stella surreptitiously watched Cass swoop down on the hostess stand, bend over and say something to Mags.

Then, menus in hand, Cass turned and beamed a hundred-watt smile at Marta Ortiz and company. She guided them past a few irate customers in line ahead of them. And while guiding the alderman and escort through the club doors, Cass managed to brush shoulders with her.

Instantly Cass seemed to jump away as if bitten. Her spine lengthened visibly.

"What's up?" came a voice from behind her.

Stella glanced back to see both Blade and Gabe behind her. "Apparently Cass just read Marta Ortiz. Whatever she got off her, it didn't look too pleasant."

"I'll be interested to hear what," Gabe said. "So far, I've got nothing on the alderman. Not that I've given up searching."

Blade cupped Stella's shoulder and gave it a gentle squeeze. He didn't say anything, didn't have to. They were on the same wavelength and always had been. She knew he would wait here with her until Cass came back.

Which took only a few minutes.

Cass's wild red hair seemed as charged as the rest of her as she whipped back to where Stella and Blade and Gabe waited. Whatever she'd sensed, it was bound to be a doozer.

"So spill," Stella urged. "What in the world did you get off her?"

Cass said, "Not a lot..."

"But something significant?" Gabe asked.

"I saw red."

"Red?" Blade echoed.

"Can you be more specific?" Stella asked.

"Blood...on her hands."

The three looked at each other in silence for a moment. Stella knew there'd been no blood associated with Tony's death, but Cass always said you couldn't take her visions at face value. She got impressions rather than specifics.

Or the blood could be someone's other than Tony's.

A death Tony found out about…the source for his blackmail?

Or a death in the immediate future?

THE IMAGE OF MARTA ORTIZ with blood on her hands stayed with Stella all the way to the South Loop. She'd decided to stay the night in Dermot's apartment, after all. She would feel closer to him there.

And, yes, safer.

Or she did until she left the garage.

The deserted street felt suffocating. As sometimes happened in this area, fog spilled over from the nearby lake—not a thick fog just yet, but a damp, cottony layer that blanketed everything in its path.

A shiver swept through Stella and she automatically felt for her weapon—for security—unsnapping the holster "just in case." Trying not to feel spooked was impossible considering her world had gone cockeyed.

Noise was muffled by the pale overlay, and lights glowed through the eerie cover with a halo-like sheen. Over on the next block, a bar with a late-night license was still open, its neon sign a smear of blue. A single car sat at the intersection, its driver waiting for the red light to change, the vehicle's beams thickly outlined by the white haze.

Other than that, she was alone.

The fog thickening before her eyes, Stella nearly jogged the quarter block to the entrance of Dermot's building. About to punch in the code to open the outer door, she almost stepped on the dark bulk laying across the stoop—some homeless guy who'd taken refuge for the night in the doorway. He was huddled against the chill and damp, his whole head ducked under a protective arm.

Great. She just *had* to deal with one more unpleasant situation before she could go inside and collapse.

"Hey, buddy, get up and move on," she said in her best cop voice.

"What's it to you, bitch?" the man mumbled, refusing to turn to look at her.

"You don't belong here."

He just grunted at her, and she had to decide whether or not she wanted to pursue the issue. Normally she would, but it had been a long, exhausting day. Too tired to hassle him or to physically remove him, she reached out to the communication box that provided security and an intercom. She punched in Dermot's code, heard the lock on the door give and opened it.

"The Garden Mission is a block over on State Street," she told the man, while trying to avoid touching him as she stepped over his inert form.

A hand clamped around her ankle and held her fast, and Stella's heart swept right up into her throat.

Then her adrenaline kicked in and so did her anger. "You don't know who you're messing with!"

As she started to turn, he jerked her foot, and though she fought it, Stella went down hard, backward, straight through the now-open doorway, where she landed flat on her back. The fall knocked the breath out of her. Even so, she rolled to the side and snaked a hand around her back toward the open holster.

But before she could pull the gun, a knife was in her face.

And behind that, a skull mask wreathed in wisps of fog.

''Hey, bitch, you never learn, do you?''

Chapter Eleven

Panic froze Stella, and she stared at the gloved hand holding the knife with a fancy handle carved into what looked like a skeleton. The blade gleaming wickedly under the foyer light was long, and the edge looked as sharp as the other time....

Only, this wasn't the other time and she wasn't the same Stella.

Sucking in air, she punctuated the breath by slashing her knee up through his legs, the contact not enough to incapacitate the bastard, but enough to make him rear back, cursing. She scooted backward and kicked out, smacking him with both feet and with enough strength that he fell off the stoop and let the knife go flying.

He was upright in a flash, but so was she. Before she could get her hand on her gun, he was on her. Strength came from somewhere—an adrenaline rush like no other, and Stella tried putting the heel of her hand straight through that damn skull mask, thinking to then grab it and reveal her attacker's identity. Even as his head snapped back, he grabbed her wrist and thwarted her. Twisting her arm behind her back, he threw her facefirst into the building. The side of her head smacking into brick stunned her.

His laugh was low and evil, his breath hot on her neck for a second before he suddenly let go. As the already hazy world spun around her, Stella was aware of him going after the knife. But stunned as she was, she was doing well to keep upright, no less doing something about stopping him.

His words gravelly and low, barely more than a whisper, the skull-face said, ''This time, you die.''

''I don't think so,'' came another male voice.

Stella forced herself to focus and pushed herself away from the building, thinking it couldn't be. But a glimpse of the man stepping out of the fog convinced her it was, indeed, Dermot.

The two men circled each other, testing each other with jabs. Then Dermot delivered a solid punch to her attacker's middle.

Skull-face came back fighting, knife swinging. He clipped Dermot's arm with the tip, but not seeming to notice, Dermot grabbed the man's knife hand and struggled for the weapon. Maybe it had just cut his jacket, Stella thought, watching them dance in circles along the sidewalk.

When they broke free of each other, the knife was in Dermot's hand.

Her attacker backed up, then charged and placed a roundhouse kick to Dermot's side that made him buckle. Stella gasped at the violent contact. Dermot dropped the knife, and it clattered against the sidewalk and spun away to disappear in the fog. Thankfully, he recovered quickly enough to repel another attack.

For a moment Stella was unable to do anything but watch Dermot in action.

Not the Dermot she knew…but the one he'd been long before she'd ever met him…the gang member who'd put a rival in a coma…the one who had surfaced to beat her rapist bloody.

The attacker came at Dermot again, and he not only blocked the kick, but grabbed and twisted the man's leg so he yelped and flipped over, hip smacking the cement sidewalk hard. He rolled into the fog—so thick now that you could barely see several yards in any direction—and before Stella could blink, skull-face came back into view, knife in his hand.

Heart pounding, she drew her gun from the holster and yelled, "Stop right there. Drop your weapon and take off the damn mask! You're under arrest!"

Skull-face took one look at the weapon in her hand, then turned and fled.

Stella aimed, took a deep breath and cursed. She couldn't do it, couldn't shoot a man in the back. She lowered her aim to his leg, but before she could make up her mind to squeeze the trigger, her attacker disappeared into the fog.

Going after him would be an exercise in futility, she knew, so she holstered her gun and swore. "Damn it!"

"Are you all right?"

She glanced at Dermot. "I'm fine," she said tightly, trying not to sound defensive.

"I thought he had you."

The trouble was, so did she.

DERMOT FIGURED that once they were inside his apartment, Stella would come down off her adrenaline high and be herself. Only it wasn't happening. She was acting weird around him, as if he'd done something wrong. He wanted in the worst way to take her in his arms and hold her, to tell her everything would be all right. But he didn't think she was in any mood for it.

Staring out the window into the fog-shrouded street, Stella said, "I never expected you to be out tonight."

"Stark's one criminal lawyer with a lot of clout. He called in a favor."

"That's good. Real good." She tossed her jacket over a chair, then removed her holster and weapon. "Otherwise you might not have made bail."

Her tone was cool, matter-of-fact, as if she hadn't almost lost her life out on the street. This was her cop demeanor, he guessed, plucked out of her resources to protect her. Lucky for her, he'd arrived when he had. He didn't want to visualize what might have happened if he hadn't.

Personally, despite the fact the guy had gotten away, Dermot was relieved that Stella wasn't hurt this time. This time he'd gotten to her before anything terrible could happen. That was something.

"So tell me exactly what went down," he said.

"I guess he must've followed me from the club. And probably from home before that. Since they impounded your car, I had to go home to get mine."

As she spoke, she became more restless and paced the living area. She seemed wired and determined to hide any emotion she might be feeling.

"You had no idea you were being followed?" Dermot asked.

"I must've been too distracted with the case. Anyhow, I left the car in the garage, and by the time I got to your front door, he was waiting for me." She laughed, the sound bitter. "I thought he was just some homeless guy bedding down in your doorway for the night."

Dermot watched her closely. She didn't seem to be in shock. She wasn't exactly angry, either. But something was going on. Disappointment, he supposed.

"So you didn't get a look at his face?" he asked.

"Afraid not. I tried to get the mask off but I just couldn't do it."

She shook her head and sounded as though she was blaming herself. Figuring the thwarted cop in her wouldn't let her relax, Dermot couldn't help himself. Against his better judgment, he tried to still her pacing by putting his arms around her.

She pushed him away. "Don't."

"Did I do something to make you angry?"

"Of course not. You did all the right things. You saved my life. Again."

It hit Dermot then—it wasn't simply that the bad guy had gotten away from her, but that *he* had stepped in. While he felt relieved and vindicated by the way the incident had played out, she wasn't taking having her life saved too well.

"Any guesses about your attacker's identity?" he asked, trying to get her away from negative thoughts. Maybe he could involve her in the details. "Manny Santos?"

She shook her head. "I don't think so. The bastard

didn't use a normal voice, but still, it didn't sound like Manny. Plus this guy was bulkier than Manny. And to tell the truth…it simply doesn't fit. The vibes were wrong. Manny had the usual bravado, but he also had some hesitation—some fear—left in him. Not this guy. He was a cold-blooded killer if I ever met one.''

''We need to make an official report.''

Her voice was even tighter when she said, ''Which means we would need to tell everything, starting with the threatening note Manny Santos left for me. Which would then get Logan into trouble since he called in a favor to have the prints pulled and matched. He's just back on the force. And now I gave him that note about Tony's death to have analyzed.'' Her shoulders slumped. ''I don't know if I can do it—screw up his career like that.''

Or her own, Dermot thought, considering repercussions that went way beyond the job.

Undoubtedly it had never occurred to Stella that helping him would put *her* in danger. He knew *he* hadn't taken the danger factor into consideration or he never would have agreed to let her back into his life.

Big mistake. But then he'd made so many mistakes in his life…

Suddenly Stella gasped. ''Dermot, your arm—it's bleeding.''

He glanced down. Crimson stained his clothing. ''So I am.''

''Take off your jacket.''

''It's nothing,'' he said, shrugging the material off his shoulder, wincing when the pain got to him.

"Here, let me."

Stella's whole demeanor changed. As she carefully slid his jacket off his arm, her expression was filled with more than worry for him. The vibes he got from her were potent, maybe a little scary for her, because she was trying to hide whatever she was feeling.

When she looked down, she sucked in her breath. "We need to get you to a hospital."

It did look pretty bad—worse than it felt. He moved his arm, and the blood pooled wider.

Even so, he said, "I have a first-aid kit in the bathroom cabinet. Don't worry, it's just a scratch. I've had a lot worse."

But the assurance didn't make her look any less pale.

The next thing Dermot knew, Stella was unbuttoning his shirt and he was forgetting about his arm. Other parts of him were taking precedence. He watched her hands work—nice hands with short nails polished a buff color. Her fingers brushed his chest and his erection hardened.

"Do you think we should just cut it off?" she asked.

Dermot started. "Cut what off?"

"The sleeve. What did you think I meant?"

He squirmed a little. "I don't think it's necessary."

"Sit still. Let's get the good arm free first, then."

There was a lot of touching in the process, and despite the cut's throbbing, Dermot didn't complain. All he could think about was having her hands all over him.

Chest…abs…lower.

After freeing his good arm, Stella leaned in too

close for his comfort as she passed the material around his back. Her heat pressed against him and her scent was so enticing he felt tortured.

A good torture. A great torture. He wanted more.

She carefully peeled the shirtsleeve down the wounded arm. He tried not to let on that the action vibrated his flesh with pain, but from the looks of her expression—her forehead pulled into a frown—Stella knew.

She gently lifted his arm to shoulder height and handed him the bloody shirt. "Keep the arm up above your heart and apply as much pressure as you can stand with that shirt, to help stop the bleeding. I'll get the first-aid kit. Any towels you don't mind losing?"

Doing as she instructed with the shirt, Dermot winced. Through gritted teeth, he said, "Take whatever you need."

She nodded. "I only wish there was something I could do to make it better."

Despite the wave of pain coursing through his arm from the applied pressure, he couldn't take his eyes off Stella as she crossed to the bathroom. He'd never before wanted a woman so much that it hurt.

And he could think of only one way she could make that hurt better.

AFTER GETTING THE SUPPLIES she needed, Stella spent a few minutes in the bathroom simply pulling herself together. So many emotions were rushing through her, she didn't know which to address first.

She wanted Dermot and, no fool, she knew he wanted her, at least for the moment. Maybe his playing her protector had turned him on.

Wrong, wrong, wrong.

Exactly what she'd feared. He was still seeing her as someone who had to be protected. She wasn't a victim anymore, and she didn't want his pity.

She wanted his love.

And then there was the actual attack. What had started as a warning two days before had turned deadly serious.

She must be making someone very nervous—nothing else made sense.

If only Detectives Norelli and Walker respected her, she could work with them on the case, give them everything she knew, see if they had something that would fill in the missing pieces of the puzzle. But she could lay it all out for them and they might do nothing. They had such contempt for her, they probably *would* do nothing.

So what were her choices?

As Stella left the bathroom with arms loaded, she figured she had to tell someone in the department what was going on, while keeping Logan out of it. Maybe Mack.

After she took care of Dermot.

His arm was still raised, the elbow resting on the back of his chair, but he'd stopped applying pressure. The bloody rag sat on the nearby counter.

His eyebrows shot up when he saw her armload. "Are you sure you left anything in the bathroom?"

"Are you sure you don't want to bleed to death?" she snapped in return.

"Touché. However, the bleeding has already stopped."

"Good. But keep the arm raised till we're done here."

Setting everything on the counter, she took a couple of the hand towels and threw them in the sink where she sprayed them with warm water. Then she began wiping the blood off Dermot. He didn't even wince when she cleaned around the wound, but when she wiped a smear of blood off his chest, he sucked in his gut, which showed off his abs.

Freezing for a second, Stella couldn't help but stare at the magnificent sight.

"The arm?" he reminded her. "I can't hold it up all night."

"Right."

Flushing with warmth, she wiped down his arm with a clean, wet towel and then opened the first-aid kit. Finding an antiseptic pad, she ripped open the packet.

"This is going to hurt you more than it will me, right?" he joked.

Stella swallowed hard. "Sorry."

He didn't so much as flinch when she dabbed antiseptic across the opening. Years of practice being macho? she wondered. Quickly cleaning the cut, she concentrated on what she was doing rather than on him. She didn't want to look at his face to see the pain she'd caused him.

Two minutes and three adhesive strips holding the wound closed later, and she let him lower his arm.

"Keep an eye on that wound. If it starts to look red and puffy, you'll have to get a professional to take care of it. You really could use a tetanus shot."

He shook his head. "Had one a couple of years ago."

"And don't do anything too strenuous."

"Like fight off another attacker?"

She felt the blood drain from her face. "Yeah, like that." She turned back to the counter and busied herself cleaning up the mess.

"Stella, don't."

"Don't what?"

"Turn away from me. I don't get it. I helped you out. So what?"

She whipped around to face him. "I'm the cop."

"And you're a tough one."

"Yeah, like you would know. I really can take care of myself." She wanted to believe she could have overcome skull-face if Dermot hadn't shown. "I'm not a victim anymore."

Dermot backed off slightly. "Whoever said you were?"

She remained tight-lipped.

"Is that the problem? You're offended because you think I believe you can't take care of yourself?"

"I'm not offended."

"And I don't believe it. The part about your not being able to take care of yourself, that is. I'm certain that if I hadn't shown up, you would have beaten the guy to a bloody pulp. And cuffed him and taken him in."

His words making her feel a little better, Stella said, "I didn't have any cuffs on me. I left them upstairs."

"Upstairs?" He looked quite interested in that information.

"Where *you're* going to sleep tonight."

He responded with a grin that made her stomach flutter.

"Alone."

He grinned harder.

"I mean it," she choked out. "Go on upstairs. I'll sleep on the couch tonight."

Dermot got off the seat and winced. "I could use some help."

Stella was at his side in a flash, putting her arm around his back. His very naked back. Her mouth went dry. And suddenly she realized he was looking down at her with a hungry expression.

"Liar," she said softly, the breath catching in her throat.

"What are you going to do about it?"

What could she do about it when his arm snaked around her waist and pulled her close? Her pulse beat rapidly in her throat.

"Say good-night here," she said.

"Another good-night kiss?" He shut out any further objections by covering her mouth with his.

Part of Stella wanted to push Dermot away, but another part wanted to pull him closer. The second part—the part that had loved him all along—won. The part that felt disappointed in herself—in needing to be rescued yet again—quieted. She would take that shortcoming out and examine it when she was alone.

For now she had Dermot.

She had his lips on her mouth, on her neck, in her hair. She had his hands along her spine, around her hips, under her bottom.

Stella's senses sang with an aliveness she'd never before felt. She could have been killed tonight—they both could have—without her ever knowing Dermot in the way a woman could know a man. But here was her chance. No doubt danger had pushed him beyond whatever he thought appropriate. He seemed as eager to prove he was alive as she.

That was it, she thought—a taste of danger was making them reckless.

He pulled her up into him and danced her around to the spiral staircase. She thought he would let her go and push her up the stairs and fling her onto the bed, but he did none of these things.

Instead he pressed her back into the steel rail and hooked both hands under her short-sleeved sweater. His hands were hard against her soft flesh. He kneaded her waist, then slid both hands down inside her slacks.

"Take them off," he murmured into her mouth.

"Here?"

"Now."

Dermot didn't stop stroking her, but kept up a rhythm that set her nerve endings on fire. It was going to happen, she thought. The very thing she'd dreamed of for so long.

Then, if she had to die, she could die happy.

She did as he commanded and unzipped her slacks. No, she wouldn't die, and neither would he. What they would do was celebrate life at least for this one night. As her slacks slid down her legs to pool at her ankles, he dipped one hand into the front of her panties.

Stella gasped when his fingers found her, hot and wet and eager for his touch. A spiraling sensation began deep within her. She managed to kick away both slacks and shoes and opened to him more fully. He plunged two fingers in deep, his thumb strumming a tune on her most sensitive part that she could almost hear in her head.

"Oh, yes," she gasped, rocking her hips so his fingers slid in and out of her.

"Touch me," he murmured.

He didn't have to urge her harder. Her hands did what he wanted, smoothing bared shoulder muscle, stroking his back, splaying across his abs. She undid his trousers and went exploring on her own, touching him so lightly with her fingertips that he groaned and shifted so he filled her hand.

She wanted him filling other places.

Jerking down his pants, she lay back against the stairs and pulled until he was within tasting distance. She took him in her mouth and slid her lips down his shaft. He tensed immediately and tangled his fingers in her hair, and she could tell he was fighting giving in to release. She nipped him lightly, then sucked.

Dermot groaned and the next thing she knew, his hands were under her arms, lifting her up several stairs so they were face to face. She pushed her panties halfway down her thighs, and he somehow managed to slide inside her. The fit was tight—both the undergarment and her. She hadn't been with anyone in a while…yet she didn't hesitate to lift her hips and urge him in farther.

He rocked into her, and the spiral staircase rocked with them, creaking as it moved. An odd sensation, she thought hazily, watching his tense expression through slitted eyes. He balanced himself over her and watched her back. She slipped her hands between them so she could struggle out of her sweater, then her bra.

Cupping her own breasts, she pushed them together and arched her back so the mounds of flesh and tightened nipples thrust toward his face.

He suckled her then, and within seconds her body tightened to fever pitch.

"Now," she murmured.

He released her breast. "Yes, now!"

Then Dermot kissed her as if he couldn't get enough of her. Stella felt him spasm inside her with a release of hot, smooth fluid.

She couldn't get enough of him...or of it.

The little death...the only kind she was willing to allow....

FUZZY-HEADED and delightfully boneless, Stella awakened practically with first light. She and Dermot had made love several times the night before, the last time in his bed. In the end, they'd shared.

She watched him sleep for a while, before her lids drifted shut again. A little more sleep and sweet dreams, she reflected, before they had to come back to reality.

Everything was about to change, she thought hazily.

She had to report the threats and the attack. She had to keep Logan out of it. No reason she had to admit the prints were already run on the note.

In just a little while...

The phone shrilled her back awake. Brilliant sunlight glowed through the high windows and streaked the bedroom area with gold, making her realize she must have slept for another hour or so.

"Dermot…"

But he was no longer there beside her. Focusing, she could hear the shower running behind the insistent ringing.

Stella stumbled out of bed and grabbed the telephone from the dresser. "O'Rourke residence."

"Stella, it's Logan."

She drew herself together and focused. "Good, I wanted to give you a heads-up. I, um, was forced to a decision last night. I need to let someone know about Manny and—"

"Manny's why I called."

A warning knot formed in the pit of her stomach. "He got himself arrested?"

"Try murdered."

"What!"

The last thing she'd expected to hear chased away any remnants of sleep.

"He was murdered sometime during the night. His body was found a couple of hours ago. You can be thankful I pulled the case."

She couldn't believe it—right after deciding she had to report Manny's actions, among other things. Stella had expected he would be brought in for questioning. He might have cracked under expert interrogation, maybe given up a name…now that would never happen.

"How?" she asked.

"Knifed. And he was wearing a skull mask."

She gasped, "Skull…" But that hadn't been Manny who'd attacked her the night before, she was certain. She might think the mask was a coincidence…if she believed in them. A sour taste rose in her mouth. "What about the murder weapon?"

"Left in him. A real collector's item, too."

Stella closed her eyes and already knew the answer when she asked, "The handle—was it white and carved to look like a skeleton?"

"How do you know that?"

"Last night a man in a skull mask tried to kill me using that same knife."

But why kill Manny?

"Okay, that doesn't make sense," Logan said. "The assumption at Area 4 is that someone from a rival gang murdered Manny. Apparently enough of them were at the Day of the Dead festivities yesterday."

"I know. We saw them. But that's not it, Logan. My instincts tell me it wasn't a gang war killing."

Stella quickly sketched out the attack for him.

As she was talking, Dermot walked into the bedroom, wearing nothing but a towel. Stella flushed and felt awkward. It wasn't supposed to be uncomfortable the morning after… Suddenly realizing that she was nude, she pulled a sheet off the bed and wrapped it around her while she explained what had happened to Dermot.

Then she turned her attention back to Logan. "Did someone contact the family?"

"Yeah. The parents are naturally distraught. And there's more good news. The kid brother, Pablo, has disappeared. No clues as to where, either."

Stella shook her head. Poor Mrs. Santos.

"Logan, I don't know what to do now. After what

happened last night, I decided to come in and make an official report about the threats and attacks without involving you, of course—I didn't need to say anything about your running the fingerprints. But now with Manny dead…''

"If that's what you want, do it. What's the problem?''

She closed her eyes and replayed part of the attack in her mind.

Skull-face fighting…knife swinging…clipping Dermot's arm…Dermot grabbing the man's knife hand…and when they broke free the knife in Dermot's hand…

When she opened her eyes it was to meet Dermot's gaze.

"There's a hitch in the plan, Logan. Dermot's fingerprints may be on the knife.''

Logan cursed, and she watched the color drain from Dermot's face.

"Then they're gonna get a match on Dermot, anyway,'' Logan said. "You know they printed him when they brought him in yesterday.''

"So we really don't have much time,'' she said.

Only until the prints got into the system.

Chapter Twelve

Dermot's situation hit him with full force. "I could be found guilty of two murders, not just one," he said, after Stella hung up the phone.

"You won't be."

She was putting on a good face, but Dermot knew it was bravado. He read her all too easily. She was taking this personally. Rather than being better off for all her and Team Undercover's work, his situation had just gotten worse and she was probably blaming herself.

Not that anyone but the murderer was to blame.

"Not making that report last night was a big mistake," she said. "Skull-face mighta been picked up before Manny was murdered."

"You couldn't have saved him, Stella. By the time anyone was looking for your attacker—"

"But maybe I could have saved you with a preemptive strike. Now if we go in with the real story…"

Stella pulled the sheet tighter around herself, covering more of her flesh, as if hiding it from him. Considering the various ways they'd made love the night before, he didn't think there was an inch of her not familiar to him. So why the sudden modesty?

Knowing she might simply be shy when not in the heat of passion—Dermot tried not to take it personally. She was distraught over the new turn of events, and he'd better concentrate on that. Getting her in cop mode was probably the best thing for her right now, even if he had other things in mind. Smelling the musky scent she hadn't yet showered off, he was turned on all over again.

"It would help to know why Manny was killed," he said, putting some distance between them. Maybe if he couldn't smell her, couldn't be tempted to tangle his fingers in her hair once more, he could get rid of the sexual buzz that was distracting him. "Maybe Manny was ready to talk. And maybe that's why Pablo disappeared—so he could protect his own hide. Maybe he even saw his brother murdered. So, if we find Pablo…"

"We get the facts? An eyewitness? All our questions answered? Yeah, right, maybe."

Stella didn't look convinced. Dermot knew there was something going on in her head. He could practically hear the wheels turning.

"Where are you going with this?" he asked.

Nope, distance didn't matter. Nor did the sheet. He had a burning desire to distract her, which was quite obvious through the towel wrapped around his hips.

Stella didn't seem to notice.

"What if skull-face meant to set you up for Manny's death?" she asked. "Why the hell else would he leave the murder weapon behind?"

"He was wearing gloves," Dermot reminded her, "so what did he care if it came with him or not?"

"Exactly. He was wearing gloves and you weren't. But that knife was a collector's item, worth a lot of money. If he left it behind, he meant to. That was no accident. It was planned. He knew your prints were on the knife handle, that you'd be held accountable."

"So you're saying it's a setup. Why?"

"He could have hated Manny, figured this was a way to get rid of him without consequences."

"Or?" Dermot knew there had to be an *or.*

"Or you were the main target and Manny was simply expendable. He could have gotten rid of someone who didn't matter to him to make sure that *you* took the fall for both murders."

"That's a big or." Big enough to deflate any inclination he might have had about getting Stella back into bed.

"I have another one."

Dermot was liking this less and less. "Give it to me."

"What if the murderer meant to set you up for Tony's death in the first place, not simply because you were convenient but because of some old grudge?"

"You mean you don't think Tony swiped my laptop—"

"No. That's not what I mean. The velvet ropes. Maybe their being stolen the night you were at St. Peter's *wasn't* a coincidence. The murderer could have been getting rid of two birds with one stone, so to speak, right from the first. Who have you pissed off lately?"

''Probably a few people...but nothing worth all this.''

''What about the past?''

''How far back?''

Although, why ask, when he knew where she was going with this. He'd been away at school, and then working in D.C. for years until recently.

''Far,'' she said. ''Something that involved you and Tony, perhaps?''

Dermot's gut tightened. Only one thing came to mind, and it wasn't something he could tell her about. It couldn't be...

But Dermot wondered if it was.

The seal of the confessional was going to follow him to his grave.

He only hoped that event didn't come sooner than nature intended.

WHILE DERMOT WENT to St. Peter's to talk to Father Padilla about Manny and Pablo Santos, Stella decided to visit her cousin Frank, bring him up to speed and see if he'd gotten any more information. She met him in the auto-parts shop, where he was still waiting for his first customer of the morning.

''I don't like this, Stella. You're gonna get hurt.''

He didn't say the obvious, that she could wind up dead.

''So what do you suggest I do—turn my back on an innocent man?''

''I'm gonna be a little selfish here and say, yeah. You're too close to this thing...''

Too close to Dermot—that's undoubtedly what he meant. And Stella was wondering if he had a point he didn't even know about. That is, she didn't think Frank realized she'd slept with the man. Whether or not that was a mistake was still to be seen. But she couldn't help but be nervous about the sudden change in her relationship with the man she loved.

"I'm committed, Frank." At least in clearing Dermot's name. She would wait and see about the other. "I'm in it for the long haul."

Her cousin shook his head but he didn't argue with her. Still, she felt his disapproval come at her in waves. She guessed she couldn't blame him. She was all he had left in the way of family, at least family living in Chicago. He didn't want to see anything bad happen to her.

She hugged him and kissed his cheek. He hugged her back. Tight.

"You always were a stubborn one, Star."

"When it comes to people I care about..."

Realizing it was almost noon and still no customers, at least not in the parts store—a couple of cars were being worked on next door—Stella wondered how much business Frank actually got these days. The shelves were dusty, as if nothing much had moved off them in a while. Considering there were now several chain auto-parts stores in the Chicago area, a lot of the little guys were being forced out of business.

Frank still lived nice, though, so he couldn't be doing too badly. Or maybe he was living off the car repair and kept the auto-parts store open because he was too stubborn to give in. That stubborn thing ran in the Jacobek family.

Coming back to the reason she was here, Stella asked, "Anything new on your front?"

"I did some checking on Louie Z."

"The poker game?"

"Not exactly. You ever wonder why Johnny Rincon never does time?"

"Because he's careful. He lets others take the blame. And then when he is arrested, things go wrong...like evidence disappearing," she said, remembering the last time he'd got off, which hadn't been all that long ago.

"Did you ever wonder where all that bad luck is coming from?"

Realizing he was implying Luis Zamora was more than friendly with a criminal—that he was actually a bad cop—she asked, "Where is this information coming from?"

"One of my mechanics picked it up somewhere."

"That's not good enough, Frank. Thirdhand gossip isn't good enough to paint a cop dirty."

Stella hated having this half knowledge, hated the fact that part of her was tempted to believe Frank.

"Okay, then forget it. I guess I don't have the connections I used to, to get you good information."

"Or maybe you're looking in the wrong direction. I imagine your contacts don't have much to do with Marta Ortiz."

"The alderman again? What have you got on her?"

"Nothing any more solid than what you have on Louie Z." Gossip she overheard by accident at the Day of the Dead festivities. "Rumor has it her political coffers might not be clean."

"Rumors usually have some basis in fact. And that

one doesn't surprise me. Can't trust a politician any
further than you can throw one. But cooking the
books and murder…they don't necessarily go together. Besides, I don't think Marta has it in her. A
little thing like her isn't strong enough to subdue and
string up a healthy young man. And you said it was
a man who attacked you last night, right?''

"Yes, but it could be someone on her payroll doing
her dirty work…or maybe even Louie Z.," she admitted reluctantly. "At the festivities yesterday—they
were huddled together, talking about something. I
thought they looked pretty cozy.''

So, was the thing they were talking about getting
rid of *her?* she wondered. Could the masked killer
have been a cop?

"I wouldn't take your eye off Johnny Rincon if I
was you," Frank said. "He and Tony weren't friendly
since Tony got out of the joint.''

"Yeah, we discussed the blackmail angle there, but
as much as I would like to pin Johnny with something, I don't think this is it." Stella let out a big
breath. "I know how to do this, so why isn't it easier?''

"'Cause it's personal. Personal makes doing things
you don't wanna do hard.''

"I guess.''

She glanced out the window again as another car
pulled up to the repair shop. "Hey, did Leroy ever
stop by?''

"Why would he do that?''

"His kids. He needs extra work to support them.''

"He can go looking for it somewhere else then!''

Stella whipped around to stare at Frank. What in

the world had Leroy done to make her normally congenial cousin so uptight? Thinking about it, she remembered Leroy hadn't been any more enthusiastic. Whatever—it was between the two of them—she guessed she ought to drop it.

The bell above the door jingled as it opened. A stocky man dressed like a mechanic wandered in, saying, "Hey, Frank, I got me a list of stuff I need here a yard long."

"Can you wait a few minutes, Clive? I was just finishing up with my cousin, the new police detective," he said, practically swaggering with pride.

"Yeah, yeah, sure." Clive busied himself looking over parts on a shelf.

Stella took that as her cue. "I need to get on my way, but if you hear anything at all…"

"You got it. Stay safe."

Frank's words rang in her ears as she left the shop. Staying safe was definitely a priority. She simply wasn't sure how to manage it.

DERMOT ENTERED St. Peter's wondering if he was wasting his time again, if the seal of the confessional would once more thwart him. No matter, he had to try.

He found Father Padilla in his office. No receptionist sat at the front desk to announce him, and the door was open, so he walked right in.

The priest looked up from his work before Dermot could even announce himself. "Dermot, another visit so soon?"

But the priest didn't sound surprised, Dermot realized. "You were expecting me."

Padilla inclined his head in answer, and Dermot studied him for a moment, wondering how much he knew. And how much he might say if carefully approached.

"I'm looking for Pablo Santos."

"His parents came to me, told me about his brother." The priest shook his head sadly. "I tried to get Manny on a different road, but the lure of being part of a powerful gang was too much to resist."

"What about Pablo?"

"He's young. He still has a chance."

"Have you heard from him?"

"If I had…" Padilla shrugged.

"Your hands would be tied."

The kid had been here, Dermot thought, or he would have gotten a definite negative on that. And he hadn't gotten a seal of the confessional speech, so maybe…

Dermot said, "I think Pablo saw Manny being murdered and now he's afraid for his life. If he could tell us what he saw, we might be able to get the killer behind bars. Then he could feel safe."

Padilla thought about it for a moment, then seemed to pick his words very carefully. "Often someone running in fear needs to find sanctuary. I'm sure you understand that concept, my son. So go, enter the church and pray for an answer. Perhaps one will be granted you."

He was being dismissed. Wanting to argue, to demand the priest tell him what he knew, Dermot held his tongue. Instinct told him Father Padilla *was* trying to tell him something without actually saying whatever he wanted Dermot to know.

"You think I should go into the church to find my answers," Dermot said, just to be sure.

The priest nodded. "Pray, my son, and have patience."

His mind spinning, Dermot left the office and went through the sacristy and toward the entrance to the church.

Often someone running in fear needs to find sanctuary....

Sanctuary as a concept...as in the church sheltering someone who needed protection? A priest wouldn't turn away anyone who sought sanctuary because he was in fear for his life. Traditionally, the priest would give him shelter, the protection of the church. Had Pablo, not knowing where else to go, asked Father Padilla for sanctuary?

Senses alert, Dermot entered the church. He stood in the doorway, and without seeming to, scanned the area around him. The interior lights were off, but sunlight shone through the stained-glass windows illuminating hundreds of floating dust motes.

He moved quietly forward and around to the congregation side of the altar. Slipping into a pew, he knelt. And he prayed to find Pablo, who would tell the truth...who would be the key to clearing his name...and he in turn would be allowed to save Pablo from following in his brother's footsteps...or to his grave.

A slight sound whispered through the church. A frightened kid hiding but getting restless?

Patience, Father Padilla had commanded.

Dermot could outlast any restless, reckless kid.

But could he make Pablo talk?

Velvet Ropes

"So, we're working with a ticking clock," Stella told the members of Team Undercover when they got together before the club opened that evening.

While waiting for Dermot to show, she'd gone over the attack on her and Manny's subsequent murder. Where the heck could Dermot be? she wondered. He'd called her cell a while ago and said he had something to show them, and that he would be here as soon as he could.

"We have maybe a few days before the prints are entered into the system," Logan explained. "Actually, it's a good thing Stella never made a report about his threatening her, or Norelli would pick up on the connection and have the prints rushed. They would have a match, and Dermot would rot in a jail cell before any judge would grant bail again."

"You can't talk to Manny, and Pablo has disappeared, so what now?" Cass asked.

Gabe said, "I've been looking more closely at Marta Ortiz." He handed Stella a folder. "She has a very interesting history…as the leader of a girl gang."

"What?" The very idea shocked Stella—an alderman who was fighting the gangs was a former gang member herself! "I know she's several years older than me, but I don't remember her being part of a gang."

"Neither do I," Blade agreed.

"That's because she wasn't originally from Pilsen or from anywhere on the south side. Try Humboldt Park."

A north side neighborhood not too far from the club and the location of the Humboldt Park Center for Change, the organization Dermot worked for, Stella thought as she looked at the information given to her. It was an old article in the *Chicago Writer,* a free newspaper that specialized in feature stories the traditional papers didn't cover. This one was about girl gangs, and there on the front page was a photo of a familiar-looking, dark-haired young woman, identified only as Marta O., leader of the Latina Queens.

"It does look like her," Stella said, "but this is dated nearly twenty years ago."

Gabe said, "Once I found that article, I followed up with a couple of calls. The *O.* stands for Ortiz."

A shocking discovery, but what did it mean? Stella wondered. Marta had been incredibly young here, and if she'd participated in criminal activities maybe young enough to have her juvy records sealed.

Before they could get into the significance of the find, a knock drew everyone's attention to the door opening. Dermot stood there, and in front of him was a terrified-looking Pablo Santos.

DERMOT HAD STAYED ON ALERT in St. Peter's for nearly three hours before Pablo had tried to sneak out from where he was hiding behind one of the side altars. Only after Pablo had made his presence known did Dermot speak to the kid, first telling him he wanted to put Manny's murderer behind bars. The kid could have run then, but where to? Where would be safer than taking sanctuary in the church? So he'd let Dermot talk. And he'd let himself be convinced that he could be the one to put his brother's murderer behind bars.

"This is Pablo Santos," he told the members of Team Undercover, knowing that Stella was already familiar with the kid. "He witnessed his brother Manny's murder last night."

"Oh, you poor thing! Come, sit. We're going to help you if you'll let us," Cass said, motherly instincts apparently coming from somewhere.

Pablo headed for the seat she offered, arcing wide to keep his distance from Stella.

Dermot was right behind him, but stopped and put an arm lightly around Stella's back. She leaned into him and he gave her a squeeze. Having so many people around, he couldn't do what he really wanted, couldn't take her in his arms for a long, deep kiss.

As if she could read his mind, Stella surreptitiously elbowed him. "So tell us," she said, her face softened by heightened color which he hoped was his fault.

"Pablo's been hiding out at St. Peter's since last night. That's where I found him."

"I'm sorry about your brother, Pablo," Gideon said. His voice hardening, he added, "I can't think of anything worse than having to watch someone you love murdered."

Pablo tilted his chin to his chest, no doubt so no one could see the tears in his eyes.

Gideon wedged a hip on his desk and looked at Pablo with compassion that seemed to go beyond everyone else's reaction. Almost as if he could empathize, Dermot thought.

"You're welcome here," the club owner told the kid. "If you want, I'll find a way to keep you safe until the bastard who killed Manny is behind bars."

Dermot didn't miss the significance of the invitation. Unless he was mistaken, Gideon meant he personally would take care of Pablo. According to Blade, Gideon mostly orchestrated the team's actions. And put up bail money, Dermot thought, thankful that the club owner had been so generous. He couldn't help but be curious about what prompted Gideon to step out of his usual role.

Stella moved closer. "Pablo, I'm sure you remember me."

For a moment the wild look returned to his eyes, but when Stella didn't yell or act threatening, he calmed down and nodded. "Yeah, the lady cop."

"The lady cop who plans on seeing your brother's murderer behind bars. Tell us what happened."

Dermot thought she sounded incredibly reasonable considering what a scare he'd helped give her.

"Manny got a call on his cell after midnight." Pablo's voice shook with emotion that he seemed to be trying to control by twisting his hands together in his lap. "I knew he was sneaking off on gang business, and I wanted to go with, but he said no…"

When his voice tapered off, Stella said, "But you followed him, right?"

"Yeah. To an alley where he met this guy still wearing his mask from Day of the Dead. They were arguing about something. Then the guy pulled out a knife and s-stabbed Manny. H-he didn't even have a chance to fight."

Pablo choked back a sob, then looked embarrassed and angry. Next to him, Cass patted his shoulder without saying anything.

"What then?" Stella asked.

"H-he took off that damn mask and covered

Manny's face and ran off down the alley. I waited till he turned the corner, then went to help my brother. T-too late. I called the cops on his cell. Then that bastard came back and saw me and I ran before he could kill me.''

''He saw your face and can identify you?'' Stella asked.

Pablo nodded.

''And what about him? You saw *his* face, right?''

''Yeah, I saw his face. Paz Falco.''

''Falco?'' Stella gave Dermot a startled look.

So she remembered—Mrs. Santos had told them Manny was influenced by the guy. Dermot thought it was too damn bad he'd been influenced to death.

''Pablo, can you describe Falco?'' she asked.

''He's clean-shaven, has short hair with Zs carved in the sides and back.''

''Zs.'' Stella sounded breathless. ''Do they kind of look like lightning bolts?''

''Exactly.''

''Sounds like you've seen the guy,'' Gabe said.

''I may have seen him working my cousin Frank on Sunday, in front of the church. Frank told me he was looking for a job, but I wonder.''

Pablo's laugh was bitter. ''Falco don't need a job. He got other ways of making dead presidents.''

Illegal ways, Dermot thought, knowing *dead presidents* was slang for money.

''What do we do now?'' Cass asked.

Logan said, ''We bring Pablo to Area 4.''

''No!'' Wild-eyed, the kid jumped out of his chair and faced Dermot. ''You swore on the Madonna you wouldn't turn me in, not till you got Falco!''

"Whoa!" Gideon said. "No one's turning you in. We'll work something out."

Logan's jaw tightened for a moment before he said, "Right. We're getting close. We'll make the case soon."

"He a cop, too?" Pablo asked.

"He is, but he's very cool." Cass patted his shoulder. "And you're our secret weapon."

Pablo calmed down, and Cass took him to the employee lounge for something to eat so the rest of them could confer.

"That sure was a stroke of luck finding the kid," Gabe said.

"I had some help." Dermot explained how Father Padilla had clued him in without actually telling him anything specific. "So how did you all make out?"

Stella handed him a folder. "Check out the story Gabe found about young Marta O., Latina Queen."

"You don't say." Dermot scanned the article. "Humboldt Park, huh? I have an in with a couple of reformed gang members from the area. As a matter of fact, there's one at the center who helps teenagers prepare for legitimate employment opportunities. Maybe tomorrow would be a good time to check in at work and see what I can find out."

"Sounds like a plan," Gideon said.

"Speaking of plans…what did you plan to do with Pablo tonight?" Dermot asked, reminding him, "The kid's only fourteen."

"I know he's a minor," Gideon said. "Has he spoken to his parents yet?"

"Done," Dermot confirmed. "He won't go home. Actually, he can't go home and be safe. I told them

I would try to talk him into going in and making a
report and let the authorities take care of him.''

''Which means he would either be returned home
or given over to Family Services.''

''What's your alternative?'' Dermot asked.

''If he was with a family member somewhere safe,
there wouldn't be a problem.''

''I'll take care of it,'' Dermot said. ''I'll call Mrs.
Santos and see if I can work out something. She's
mourning one son and wants to see the other safe.
She'll cooperate.''

The club was already busy, especially since today
was Halloween. Cass poked her head in and reported
throngs of costumed customers filling the stairs, waiting to get in. The team scattered and got to work.

Dermot made the call. And within fifteen minutes
he had the solution. He'd pick up an older cousin
outside of the neighborhood who would Pablo-sit at
Gideon's place.

Hopefully, a couple of days would be long enough
to bring down Paz Falco and whoever was pulling his
strings.

THINGS WERE HEADED in the wrong direction.

Falco had failed in his mission and had taken out
his frustration on one of his own. Not that Manny
Santos was a big loss. But at least he'd done what
he'd been ordered to do and hadn't taken actions that
would bring the spotlight down on them all.

Stella Jacobek was still the key. And, regretfully,
she was still alive. Once she was out of the picture,
the operation would be back to normal. No one believed her theories, at least no one who mattered.

And no one really cared about a dead gang member. Besides, according to Falco, the only prints on the knife were O'Rourke's. And O'Rourke was still poised to take the fall on the Vargas murder. So he would go down for two. Those prints would seal his fate.

If no one messed things up.

Like Stella Jacobek.

This had to be done right, though. The blame had to go elsewhere.

A simple phone call would get the ball rolling, would set the scene so that, when she died, it would be in public, and the authorities wouldn't know who to blame.

Some things—if you wanted them done right—you just had to do yourself.

Chapter Thirteen

Dermot dead-bolted the loft door behind them. "Alone at last."

"And amazingly without incident," Stella added, wondering if their luck was changing. "Everything went as planned and Pablo is safe, assuming he stays put. No one followed us. No one tried to attack me...."

Dermot slipped his arms around her and nuzzled her neck, sending a flush of excitement straight down to her toes. "I wouldn't let anyone hurt you."

The sizzle fizzled a bit. "Yeah, right."

"But I know my interference wouldn't be at all necessary, because you're a kick-ass cop who can take care of not only herself but the whole damn city."

She flattened a hand against his chest and pushed at him. "Now you're patronizing me."

"Maybe just a little."

He was smiling at her, not only with his lips but his eyes. Stella's heart fluttered in her chest. She wanted to be as close to Dermot as she could get, but maybe that was a mistake. Their circumstances threw them together, and danger had become something of an aphrodisiac.

She wasn't sure that was healthy.

Wasn't sure if it was real.

Moving out of Dermot's arms, she said, "I wonder if we're doing the right thing, keeping Pablo hidden rather than bringing him in." She wanted him alive, not only because he was a witness, but because she'd seen something in the young gang member to salvage.

"What would you get without Pablo's cooperation?" Dermot asked. "And the next time he runs, who knows what could happen? Besides, Manny's murder is Logan's case, and Pablo's parents are in the loop and cooperating, so we're covered."

"Let's just hope nothing goes wrong with the plan. I wish it wasn't so late. I could call Frank and ask him about Paz Falco."

"Just because they were talking doesn't mean Frank has the score on Falco."

"Maybe not, but odds are he'd give me some clues as to where I could look for him."

"In the wee hours of the morning."

"Now is when he'll be on the move. Besides, there is no inappropriate time for a cop, Dermot."

He raised his eyebrows. "I'm not trying to minimize what you do or overprotect you. Well, maybe the last, but I can work on that."

And maybe her fears were for nothing, Stella thought.

Not that she knew exactly how Dermot felt about her. It was obvious that he cared for her. He wanted to protect her.

But did he love her?

Dermot's lips brushing hers kick-started her libido, making it difficult to remember she'd ever had objections to their being together. Nothing wrong with him backing her up if it proved he cared.

Dermot was showing her now, his hands spreading warmth that pulsed through Stella. All she could think about was feeling him naked against her. For a few hours she wanted to lose herself in him and forget about everything else.

Morning and Paz Falco would come soon enough.

PAZ FALCO was nowhere to be found.

A frustrated Stella was wasting her time on the hunt for him while Dermot was busy trying to track down someone who had known Marta Ortiz when she was a Latina Queen.

Despite Pablo's disbelief that Falco needed or wanted a job, Frank had insisted it was so when she'd finally called him. Supposedly Paz Falco had quit school and wanted to work full-time…or so he'd told Frank.

Why would a gang member want a job at the auto repair shop? Stella wondered, looking for a deeper motive. Maybe he thought he could scam the business somehow. Odd that he hadn't followed up with Frank since Sunday, then.

While Frank didn't know where Falco lived, he did have several suggestions as to where she might look. But the gang's haunts were deserted. Any gang members not in school were probably still sleeping.

The plan was for her to track down Falco and then call Logan for backup. Unless Logan found him first, which meant he would call her. He and his partner were working on the case day and night. The moment Falco was collared, Logan would bring Pablo out of hiding, round up his parents and get his story officially signed, sealed and delivered. The fact that a known gang member had attacked her—a cop—with intent to kill would go against him when it came to setting bail.

Stella hoped to see him rot in hell.

The trick was in finding Paz Falco. Who, other than Frank, had so many sources?

Wondering if Leroy could help her out, she called him at Lion Auto where he'd been a mechanic since leaving Frank's employ. Today was his day off. Knowing he spent much of his leisure time playing poker—perhaps one of the reasons he needed a second job—Stella headed for Skipper's.

Leroy was just getting up from the poker table when she walked into the bar. She waved to him, but seeing her didn't change his down-in-the-mouth expression. He must have been losing, she guessed.

"Stella."

"So, how's it going? No luck finding a second job?"

"Not around here. And don't tell me to see Frank again."

There was that hostility again. "What is it between you two?"

"Let's say I didn't agree with his way of doing business and leave it at that."

Now her curiosity was really whetted, but she wouldn't press him for past history when she had a kid's future—and ultimately Dermot's and her own—to think about.

"Let's go over there," she said, indicating a corner where they could talk without being overheard.

"So, how's it going?" Leroy asked in a low voice.

"Complicated, but coming along. There's someone who holds the key to the whole thing." It had become second nature to her to only reveal as little as possible to get what she needed. "Does the name Paz Falco ring any bells?"

Leroy whistled. "Only bad ones. Even other Vipers are scared of him. He's a loose cannon, doesn't answer to anyone. No one to mess with."

He answered to someone, probably Marta Ortiz.

"You wouldn't have an address on him, would you?" Stella asked.

Leroy shook his head. "I think he lives somewhere near the river, west of Ashland. How important?"

Okay, so she had to tell him. "A matter of life or death. Maybe mine."

Leroy's eyes went wide. "Give me a couple of hours and I'll try to get more specific."

Stella gave Leroy her card with her cell number. "Any leads, I'd be grateful."

Leroy approached the bar to pay his tab.

Stella left, wondering what next. She was so involved in her thoughts as she walked down the street that she didn't see Johnny Rincon until he stepped in her path, a roadblock to her car. Wearing sunglasses, as usual, his scar fully revealed, his face looked as scary as any Day of the Dead mask.

"You never learn, do you, Stella?"

The familiar sentiment clenched her stomach in a knot. "Learn what?"

"That I'm the go-to man."

"And what should I go to you for? All right, I'll give it a shot. How about telling me where I can find Paz Falco." If Johnny wasn't the one behind the attack on her and Manny's murder, he might give her a clue.

Johnny smiled. "I was thinking about something a little more personal."

Trying to breathe normally, she asked, "Like what?"

"How about…the truth about that ex-priest you're banging."

"He didn't kill anyone."

Impatiently Stella tried shouldering past him, but Johnny blocked her again.

"I'm not talking about murder." Johnny paused, then dramatically added, "O'Rourke *knew.*"

"Knew what?"

"About *you.* That you needed a lesson in keeping your mouth shut and we were gonna provide it."

Now her heart was thundering. He was talking about the past. About what happened twelve years ago. About her being raped as a life lesson.

"Dermot couldn't have had a heads-up."

"Tony knew."

"Ahead of time?"

Johnny smirked. "We all knew. We drew straws to see who would get the honor. But Tony was squeamish. Violence made him sick. He was too much of a coward. And a squealer. He needed to get what he knew off his conscience so he could live with himself. What better way than unburdening himself in the confessional?"

They drew straws. Stella was constantly amazed at
the cruelty that seemed to be inbred in some people.

"You don't know that Tony confessed anything,"
she said.

"Are you sure?"

"If Dermot had known, he would have—"

"Saved you? I guess he did try in his own pathetic
way."

Stella gasped. Dermot *had* saved her…if not from
the rape. But he'd just happened to be walking down
the street, passing the alley when…

Stella's heart thumped, and she felt as if she'd just
swallowed lead. Had Dermot known ahead of time?

"You have a good day." His grin making him look
like pure evil, Johnny Rincon shoved past her.

And Stella felt as if she was going to be sick.

DERMOT CHECKED his voice mail on the way home.
Stella had left a message, asking him to meet her at
his place as soon as possible, but there was no excitement in her voice, no indication that she'd gotten
a lead on Falco. Just the opposite. He heard a slight
waver, as if she were upset about something. Dermot
only hoped nothing had gone wrong with Pablo. He
called to find out, but she didn't pick up.

By the time he got to his neighborhood, he was as
tense as she'd sounded. And by the time he got to his
floor, he was prepared for the worst—what if Stella
had gotten hurt?

But when he opened the door to the loft, she was
sitting at the counter, as calm as you please, having
a mug of coffee. She turned to face him, and he anx-
iously scanned her form. She looked fine physically.

But her face was pale and closed, as if she'd received a shock.

"What's going on?" he asked, crossing the living area. "Did something happen?"

"You could say that."

"Did Falco—"

"Not Falco. I didn't find him."

"Then what?"

"You," she said softly.

"Me?"

A shiver of apprehension ran through Dermot. He tried to take Stella in his arms, but she simply twisted out of his grasp and moved away.

"Stella?"

"You knew," she said, her tone accusing.

Dermot clenched his jaw. "You need to be more specific."

"You knew that I was going to be raped." She pronounced each word carefully. "You knew because Tony couldn't stand having it on his conscience. He confessed to you before it even happened."

How the hell had she found out? Dermot wondered, then realized chatty Tony had shared with someone who'd shared with Stella.

"Anything Tony told me was under the seal of the confessional." Even now he couldn't talk about it.

"You're not going to defend yourself and tell me Johnny was lying?"

He didn't respond.

"I don't understand. You knew a crime was going to be committed. You knew I was going to be raped. You even knew where. That's how you found me. I was so grateful to you for saving me…when you could have stopped the rape before it happened. You could have called me and warned me." When he didn't respond, she asked, "Or did Tony wait until the last minute to make the confession? Why didn't you call the police? They could have gotten a squad to that alley faster than you could get yourself there."

His voice tight, Dermot said what he could. "Under the seal of the confessional, a priest can't repeat any part of what he hears, not for any reason, not even to prevent a crime, not even to save lives. I took a vow. I made a promise to keep what I heard to myself. I may not be perfect, but I keep my promises."

He would promise her anything now if it would make a difference, but he suspected it wouldn't. He suspected what he'd known all along—that her finding out would be the end of them. He'd known it from the first, the reason he'd been reluctant to get romantically involved with her. He couldn't be honest about this one thing, and it was this one thing that was most important to her.

Stella was staring at him as if she'd never seen him before. "I don't understand. After…knowing…how could you live with yourself?"

"I couldn't," he admitted. "I skirted the spirit of the canon when I went looking for you myself, but—"

"It wasn't enough," she finished for him.

"And I'll always regret it."

"Tony came to you so that you would do something."

"Tony came to me to be forgiven."

Tony Vargas had wanted to absolve himself of guilt

and let his confessor wear it for him, Dermot thought. Tony hadn't been any hero. He'd vowed to go straight, but he was weak, always seeking approval from his peers even as he sought forgiveness. Years later, after he'd gotten out of jail, he'd enthusiastically used Dermot's counseling services at Heartland—another form of seeking forgiveness—but he'd never changed. He was a thief to the end, as the laptop attested.

"You're not a priest anymore," Stella said. "You've had all the chances in the world to tell me the truth. You've had twelve years. You've had the past week."

"I'm still bound by the seal," Dermot said, knowing she wouldn't understand. He'd known that all along, of course. "What I *can* tell you is that what happened to you was the final straw in my so-called vocation. I never heard another confession after that."

The truth was finally out. It lay between them like an open wound.

Would it ever heal? Dermot wondered. Would this be the last time they would share a private conversation? If so, then she needed to hear the whole truth. She might not accept it, but he needed to tell it.

"So, what now?" she asked.

"That's up to you, Star. Know that you're in my heart and always have been. Know that I love you with everything I am."

She turned even whiter, if that was possible.

"I'm committed to freeing you," Stella choked out, "but after that? Don't expect me to excuse you. I'm sorry, too, Dermot, because there are some things that simply can't be forgiven."

TRYING TO PRETEND nothing was wrong, Stella primped in the ladies' lounge at Club Undercover just before opening. But her hands were trembling, and when she tried to put on her lipstick, she smeared the color over the edge of her lip.

Cursing softly, she used a tissue to remove the excess before trying again.

"So, why is this a particularly bad day?"

Stella's head jerked up and she met Cass's worried gaze in the mirror. "I just want it to be over."

"The search for justice…or you and Dermot?"

"That obvious, huh?"

"To me, yes."

Wondering how much Cass could sense, Stella said, "Nothing new happened today except that I learned what a fool I've been."

Cass sat on the stool next to her. "Do you want to talk about it?"

"What good would talking about something that happened twelve years ago do?"

"I see."

"I doubt you do."

Even if Cass could "see" the rape, she wouldn't have a clue as to Dermot's betrayal.

"You hold Dermot responsible for something that happened to you."

"Good guess."

"Something that wasn't his fault."

Stella needed to talk to someone about this. Another woman. She'd never talked to her mother or sister about what happened to her. But Cass was here, and Stella didn't know a warmer or more caring person.

"Twelve years ago, I was raped." Stella figured Cass probably guessed that part the other day. "Tony Vargas confessed the crime to Dermot before it happened. Dermot didn't call the police. He could have stopped it with one phone call, but he didn't."

Cass asked, "Are you certain the phone call would have changed the outcome?"

No, she wasn't certain. Having been on the streets in uniform, she knew how tied up the other officers in the squad might have been. "At least I would have had a chance to get away."

"Or maybe not. Dermot didn't abandon you, Stella," Cass said. "He tried to help you, but he couldn't. He's suffered, too. I've felt the darkness of his soul. He's tortured by what happened."

"Tortured?"

"With guilt."

"He should be."

"Don't be so hard on him. I think you know that Dermot is a man of honor. He was torn between what he wanted to do and the vows he took. There was no right or easy decision for him. So he tried to be true to both the church and you in the only way he knew how."

She hadn't said anything about vows getting in the way. "Did he tell you about it?"

"He didn't have to." Cass smiled. "Some things I just know about people. Give yourself some time and you'll see things more clearly." She patted Stella's shoulder. "Everyone's waiting on us. Well, everyone but Logan."

Stella nodded. "Manny's murder." She knew Logan, too, was still trying to track down Falco.

...the only way he knew how...

Cass was probably right about that. Dermot had done his best. He'd put himself on the line. He'd simply been too late. So why didn't that make a difference to her?

Stella wished she could say Cass's pep talk had done her some good, but even though she conceded Cass had a few points, Stella really didn't feel any better. It was too much to take in without stopping to think about it all, and she was determined not to stop until this case was solved.

So she took a deep breath and followed Cass into the employees' lounge. The first person she spotted, of course, was Dermot.

No matter what he'd done—or hadn't—she still loved him. Wonder of wonders, he'd said he loved her.

That made the heartbreak all the worse.

DERMOT FELT THE AIR crackle with tension when Stella entered. She paused for a moment, her gaze connecting with his. Then she skirted him to get to the coffee. Her spine was straight and she didn't look his way again. He, on the other hand, couldn't get enough of her. Considering her feelings, he might never see her again once they ended this fiasco.

Maybe he should end it, simply release her from her promise to clear his name. She would never do it, though. She had a sense of honor that would keep her working for him until the bitter end.

"Pablo and his cousin are staying safe at my place today," Gideon began. "But tomorrow, Pablo wants to make a public appearance to eulogize his brother."

The next day being the final Day of the Dead, Dermot thought.

"He can't," Stella said. "It's too dangerous for him."

"His mind's made up."

That ticking clock just started ticking faster. He could see the worry in Stella's face replace whatever else was going on in her head. Always she put others before herself. Twelve years ago she hadn't pressed charges because of the threat to her sister, Anna. And now she was forgetting her own heartache in deference to Pablo.

How could he ever make up his failure to her?

"So, any new developments?" Gideon asked.

"I couldn't find Falco," Stella said. "And so far, neither have the men Logan put on it. I'm going out again when we're done here tonight."

"Not alone," Dermot said. Thinking they could use as much street-savvy backup as they could get, he asked, "Blade, any chance you can get out of here?"

"Boss?"

"No objections."

If Stella wanted to object, she was holding herself back in tight-lipped silence. No doubt she couldn't stand to be around him anymore. But no matter how she felt about him now, she was doing this for him and he wasn't about to let her go into danger alone.

"What about your trip to Humboldt Park?" Gideon asked, interrupting his thoughts. "Did it pan out?"

"It did, though I'm not sure it helped us. I talked to one of my colleagues who was a former Latin King. Gus ran with Marta twenty years ago."

"Was Marta O. as tough as the *Chicago Writer* article indicated?"

"Tougher. Then her nine-year-old brother Jaime was killed and her world changed."

"Brother?" Gabe echoed. "Where did he come from? I only got the goods on two sisters."

Dermot realized Gabe probably hadn't heard the details of Marta's eulogy, so he hadn't known there'd been a brother who'd been killed. "Because Jaime's last name was Doral, not Ortiz. Different father."

"How did he die?"

"Drive-by. He and his friends were playing on the sidewalk, and apparently a gang member who didn't belong in the part of the neighborhood run by Latin Kings and Latina Queens was walking down the street. Marta's boyfriend was riding shotgun in a car cruising the neighborhood. Only, when he fired, he missed the gang member and shot the kid."

"How tragic," Cass murmured.

A fact of life in gang-infested neighborhoods, Dermot knew. "Marta heard the shots and ran out of the building to try to save Jaime. She screamed for help and literally tried to hold back the blood."

"But the wound was fatal," Stella said with assurance, as if having heard this story too many times. "There was nothing she could do. The moment the boy was hit it was over. It just took a few minutes for him to let go."

"The blood," Cass said. "That was the blood I saw on Marta's hands."

Dermot nodded. "According to Gus, Marta was never the same after that. She went wild with grief, all the more so because she couldn't demand a vendetta—it would have been against one of her own. Actually, her own boyfriend. After Jaime was buried, she fought her way out of the gang and started on a course to end gang violence by becoming part of the political system that could change things.''

''She's not the one, then,'' Stella said.

Gabe countered, ''That information doesn't necessarily clear her.''

''I think it does,'' Stella argued. ''Her eulogy for Tony was highly political. I don't think it was lip service. She wants to bring down the gangs, not perpetuate them, so why would she hire a member of a gang to do her dirty work?''

Everyone agreed that made sense.

''So it's between Johnny Rincon and Louie Z.,'' Stella said, and then to Gabe, ''I need a look at that file you've been compiling on Tony's murder.''

''Sure thing.''

He immediately went to fetch it for her. She only glanced Dermot's way once before getting her hands on the folder.

Dermot watched Stella thumb through it. She stopped to read something more carefully. Her forehead pulled into a frown, and Dermot wondered what she'd found.

Then her cell phone rang.

''Jacobek here.''

After listening for a few seconds, Stella stood so quickly that she knocked the folder off the table onto the floor, where it lay open to the article she'd been reading. Dermot bent to pick it up.

''That was Logan,'' she said. ''They've located Falco in an apartment building in west Pilsen. He's heading there now with some men. I'm going to meet him for the takedown."

"I'm with you," Dermot said, glancing down at the item in the folder that had held her so fixated.

Tony Vargas, holding up his prized walleye for the camera, stared back at him.

Chapter Fourteen

Stella flipped on the portable siren and the light she'd just secured with Velcro onto her dash, and headed for the capture scene. As she careened around traffic and took a hard left, a quick glance in her rearview mirror assured her Blade was keeping up.

"Watch out for that van!" Dermot said, his voice tight over the siren's wail.

"I'm not blind." Stella smoothly moved out of the van's way. "I don't need a second driver." Her nerves were tight enough as it was. Tighter since he'd opened the passenger door and had hopped in without permission. If she hadn't had to put on her Kevlar vest, he never would have gotten the chance. "You shouldn't even be in this car."

"This is about me—"

"Not anymore...not just you. It's about a gang member trying to kill a police officer and then succeeding with one of his own."

"But he may be the one who murdered Tony Vargas."

Gripping her steering wheel harder, Stella only

hoped he was right. ''But since this is going to be an official bust, you have no place there.''

Dermot had forced his way into her car, and Stella told herself she'd let him because she hadn't had any spare time to argue. She figured he would argue now—tension came off him at her in waves—but he kept his mouth shut.

Good. They didn't need to talk. They'd done enough talking. And other things. She didn't need to be distracted from her purpose.

But as she raced to end this thing, she couldn't help but regret that it would soon be over. Not regret that Dermot's name would be cleared, but that she would probably never see him again.

''Do you hate me now?'' he suddenly asked.

''Hate is a strong word.''

''So is love.''

Stella laughed. ''Love is an illusion. You see in a person what you wanna see.''

''No one is perfect, Star. All we can do is our best.''

Tears bit at her eyes, but she refused to acknowledge the sign of weakness.

All we can do is our best...

Hadn't Dermot done his best, given his circumstances? He'd tried to save her the best way he could without contravening the seal of the confessional.

I made a promise to keep what I heard to myself...I do keep my promises...

Dermot's words echoed in her head. He'd taken a vow and he'd been true to it, just as he'd been true to her afterward. Fearing for her younger sister, she'd made him promise never to tell anyone about her rape, and he never had. The truth of that struck her heavily.

Cass had said Dermot was a man of honor, who stood by his word, and she'd been correct.

Something to think about.

Only not now. Later.

After this was finished.

They were close. As she turned onto 18th Street, Stella went into stealth mode by cutting off the siren, and in another block upon turning, did the same with the light. Though it was late, pockets of the neighborhood were still alive, celebrating Day of the Dead with sparklers and illegal fireworks. A block down, she glanced into the rearview mirror, slowed and watched Blade do the same behind her. Then she kept an eye out for Logan and his men. Spotting them about a block ahead, she looked for the first clear spot at the curb. Parking, she flew out of the car just as Blade slid into the spot behind her.

When Dermot tried to follow, she said, "Stay put—this is an official operation!"

She ran to join Logan, only once glancing over her shoulder to make certain Dermot did as she ordered. He wasn't looking happy about it, but he was still standing next to the open car door, staring after her as Blade joined him. She tried to put him and the truth and the past all out of mind and concentrate on the capture. Waves of tension rushed at her from Logan and the uniformed officer with him.

Logan asked, "You brought O'Rourke along for the ride?"

"He brought himself. Blade followed."

"I hope they have sense enough to stay out of the way."

He gave her a quick rundown. Paz Falco was in a third-floor apartment of the multiunit building on the corner. Logan had stationed men on the side and in back, so when he went in the front way to make the arrest, other possible exits would be covered.

"I hope you told them we need Falco alive," she said.

"We always need them alive. Whether or not we can keep him that way…"

She knew they had to protect themselves. No cop she knew wanted a notch on his gun, but sometimes it happened, anyway. Not this time, though. Too much rested on taking the offender in alive.

They couldn't lose Falco. They needed more than a conviction. They needed information about Tony Vargas—namely, who was behind that murder. She had a growing notion, but she wanted him to tell her that her instincts were wrong. But how would she get to the truth? She hated cutting deals with cold-blooded killers…but she had to know for sure.

She had to clear Dermot.

She kept her promises, too.

"Everyone set?" Logan spoke softly into his radio. And when he got responses from both of his teams, he said, "We're going in."

Instinct kept Stella from going in with him. She waved him off and jogged around back, opening her jacket to make sure her ID and star were in plain view on her belt to the uniformed officers on the side street. Hitting the alley, she drew her weapon and stopped to stare up at the back porch, where another plain-clothes detective and a uniform were positioned in case Falco made a break through the back door.

The *bam-bam-bam* at the front door echoed through the apartment and out an open rear window, followed by Logan's muffled shout. "Police, open up."

Then nothing.

Holding her breath, Stella stared at the back door until a furtive movement caught her eye.

A crash from inside was followed by a lot of yelling, and the other detective and uniform were going in the back way.

A rocket went off, lighting up the sky with gold shards, and Stella saw Falco's silhouette. He was escaping across the roof, with what looked to be a gun in hand. She moved parallel with him as he jumped from the bigger building's roof to that of a three-story apartment building. She wanted in the worst way to yell out his position, but she feared Falco would do something desperate if she did.

She wasn't ready to die yet.

A teenager and a younger kid were messing around in the alley, ready to set off a bottle rocket. They saw her and froze. She put a finger to her lips and waved them off with her gun hand. They slipped into the shadows and disappeared.

Staying with him from the alley, she watched him make his way over the roof. He ran crouched, head down, and zigzagged forward as if he was part of some military operation. A scary thought—if all gang members were that well trained, the police would be in real trouble with them.

Falco stopped and stared down at the next roof,

which was a floor lower. Stella held her breath as he prepared to jump. He had to make it. If he killed himself, he couldn't talk. And if he couldn't talk...

He landed on the edge and swayed backward but caught himself before he went over.

Stella let out her held breath.

And as he swung himself down and onto the back porch, her heart began to pound. He was planning on coming down the stairs, and from the looks of things—one of Logan's men was just now coming out of the corner building and he was looking in the wrong direction—it was up to her to get Falco cuffed.

Sliding around the garage and keeping to the shadows, she focused on the sounds around her. Falco didn't try to cover the light slap of his footsteps as he descended the stairs. She was in the yard now, between the garage and a tree. She couldn't be sure he would come this way, but if she tried to take him in the open, he could shoot her or escape. Surprise was her best bet. Even so, the next fifteen seconds were the longest she'd ever waited.

Then he was off the porch and headed toward her. Stella whirled into the open, facing him, both hands on the weapon she pointed at his chest.

"Stop, Falco!" she yelled loud enough for Logan and his men to hear. "And drop the gun!"

"You think you can pull the trigger faster than me?"

They were facing each other, and before she could step forward, he raised his gun so they were practically barrel to barrel. Stella didn't wait to think. She grabbed his gun hand and shoved it hard to the side as she moved into him, gun first, barrel into his ribs.

An explosion made her start, and for a second she thought his gun had fired. For another second she thought the noise was simply that of a rocket being set off. Eerie red glowed along his features, illuminating his surprised expression. Then the light went out, snuffed like a candle, and he slumped against her, his weapon hitting the ground before he did.

Someone had shot Falco!

Relief that she was safe warred with terror that Falco might not be alive to talk. That everything she and Team Undercover had done would be for naught and Dermot would be screwed. Wondering who had fired that shot, she dropped down to the sidewalk next to Falco, yelling, "Call the paramedics!" and heard someone repeat her request into his radio.

Footsteps smacked the pavement around her, assuring Stella reinforcements were at hand. Not that she needed them. Falco wasn't going anywhere. For all she knew, he was dying before her eyes.

As she made the arrest and read Falco his rights, Stella found the hole in his chest and applied pressure to stop the flow of blood…just like Marta Ortiz must have done in trying to save her little brother.

"Falco, talk and we'll make a deal."

He coughed, and blood bubbled over his lips. "Too late for deals."

"The paramedics will be here in two minutes," she said, hoping that was true. "They'll save your sorry ass and then we'll put it on trial. So talk and make things easy on yourself." If he died, his confession would undoubtedly hold up, as well, and with the other officers around her, she had witnesses. "We know you killed Manny Santos and Tony Vargas—"

"Not Vargas...not mine."

Not expecting that, Stella demanded, "Who, then? Who killed Tony Vargas?"

"Think...you'll know..." His voice faded and his eyes closed.

"Bastard! Don't you dare die on me!"

A pair of legs stopped in front of her. Dermot crouched at Falco's head. He hadn't stayed where she'd told him to.

Dermot slipped two fingers along the front of Falco's throat, then nodded. "I don't know how long he has, but for now he's still alive."

A SIREN SPLIT THE NIGHT as the ambulance careened down the alley and stopped yards away from where Dermot stood looking down at Stella, who was still forcing Falco to live with the gift of her hands and, he swore, by her sheer will.

So Paz Falco hadn't killed Tony Vargas. Dermot swore silently, not wanting to upset Stella further. He'd been counting on the gang member being the one. And he didn't like the fact that Falco had put it on Stella to find the answer. That's all she'd been doing—looking for answers. Why couldn't Falco have simply given her a name?

The paramedics were on Falco then, and Stella rose and stepped away. Her hands were covered with his blood. She stared at them as if she were in shock.

"Water?" Dermot asked.

"A couple of bottles in the back of the ambulance."

Dermot jogged to the alley to get one, and when

he returned to the yard, Logan and Blade were with Stella.

Logan clapped Stella on the arm, saying, "Good work, Jacobek," sounding in good spirits despite the fact that he would not only have to explain Stella's presence at the scene to his sergeant, but would have to give her credit for the arrest.

"Water," Dermot said, joining them and holding the opened bottle out. "Give me your hands, Star."

She did so without saying anything. And without looking at him.

Dermot let the water flow over her palms and rubbed at them with his own fingers to eradicate every speck of red. Touching her filled him with such emotion that he had to steel himself lest his own hands begin to shake. Suddenly she pulled her hands away as if she couldn't tolerate the feel of him for one more second.

"We still didn't get what we need, though," Stella said as the paramedics lifted Falco, who was strapped down to a board, an IV in his arm. "I didn't get a name outta him."

"We will," Logan assured her, following the progress as the medics got Falco to the ambulance. Then he turned and looked at the men who were part of the operation. "In the meantime, which one of you fired on the offender?"

A chorus of "not me" filled the night.

"No one discharged a weapon here?"

At least no one who would admit to it.

Dermot realized Stella's attention had shifted upward. She was scanning the upper levels and rooftops of the buildings around them...looking for what?

Then it hit him that if the police officers hadn't fired on Falco, someone else had.

She was looking for that someone.

So when she ran down the alley to her car, he chased after her. "I'm coming with you!"

"No, you're not."

Stella slid into her seat behind the wheel, but when Dermot tried to open the passenger door, he found it locked.

He pounded on the window. "Stella, let me in!"

"This is something I need to do alone!"

Sick with worry for her, Dermot looked around and saw Blade talking to Logan, exiting the alley together.

He yelled, "Blade—keys!"

Blade took in the situation as Stella charged away from the curb. He tossed the keys to Dermot, who got into the SUV. A block behind her, he tried catching up to Stella. But when she turned onto a main street, other cars got between them. With each block, the distance between them grew a car length or two. Luckily he was sitting high and could see when she turned down a side street.

But traffic jammed for an interminable moment, and when Dermot made the turn, Stella's car was out of sight.

STELLA WAS SICK INSIDE. She knew. She hadn't wanted to believe it, but the proof had been in her hands barely an hour ago. And though he hadn't named names, Falco had confirmed her worst fear.

She should have looked at the contents of the damn folder Gabe was building before today. If she had, Manny Santos might still be alive.

What the hell kind of detective was she?

Tony Vargas holding up that prized walleye had been the giveaway.

She pulled into the auto-parts lot and waited. It wouldn't be long, she knew. Frank had probably parked a couple of blocks over from where he'd been waiting to shoot Paz Falco. He would have to sneak through the night to avoid being held for questioning.

How had he known? she wondered. Who had leaked the information that Falco was about to be arrested? No doubt Frank meant to silence his henchman before he could talk.

A few moments later an old Jag pulled into the lot and Frank Jacobek got out.

Opening the door, she called out, "Frank," and gave him a wave like nothing was wrong. Even so, his footsteps toward her appeared heavy and slow.

Firecrackers in the alley made them both start. Her stomach was already sick and knotted, her breathing irregular.

"Star, what're you doing here this time of night?"

"What were you doing out?" she asked, the words sticking in her throat. "Where were you tonight, Frank?"

"I don't think I have to answer to you, young lady."

He tried to make a joke of it, but she heard the tension in his voice.

"I think you do, Frank. It breaks my heart, but you have a lot of answering to do."

"I don't know what you're talking about."

He tried to move past her, but she grabbed his arm and whipped him around so his back was against her car. She hadn't even known she would be strong enough. Amazing thing, adrenaline.

"The keys, Frank. Open your trunk."

She watched him with an eagle eye as he rummaged through his pants pockets. She was ready to pull her weapon if she had to. But all he produced were the keys. Without saying a word, he walked over to the Jag with her following close, and opened the trunk.

The rifle he'd used to shoot Paz Falco lay there, mocking Stella.

How could she have been so blind…

"I was just trying to protect you, Star," Frank wheedled. "I didn't want to see you hurt again like last time."

Again? He knew about the rape? Of course he did. He knew everything that went on in the neighborhood, because he made it his business to know.

"When did you buy it, Frank?" she asked sadly, then looked him in the eye. The streetlights cast deep shadows on his face, making him look his age. Older. "When did you buy the house overlooking Lake Geneva?"

She'd seen the photograph on his wall, and she hadn't thought anything of it.

"I don't know what you're talking about."

"Sure, you know the house we picked out all those years ago on a family vacation at your cabin. Our fantasy house we were gonna buy if we ever won the lottery. How much did that property set you back when you bought it? It's gotta be worth a couple of million now."

Frank looked impressed. "You've turned out to be

a good little detective. How did you find out about the house?''

.''The walleye Tony Vargas caught. The photo for the local paper. You shouldn't have let them take it in front of the house, not when you were standing there, the proud owner on his patio.''

He cursed and said, ''That doesn't prove anything.''

''How did you buy it, Frank? Not from running the auto-parts and repair shop. You used to have more business, true, but never enough to buy that property. Tell me the truth and I'll try to help you.''

Frank laughed and the sound was icy—foreign to her—laced with a cruelty that made her shiver. Something about the feeling was familiar from when she was young. The disciplinarian. She remembered him.

''I should have taken care of Tony Vargas the first time he opened his mouth about my business!''

Heart in her throat, she asked, ''Then you admit you had something to do with his death?''

''He got himself up on the chair and put the velvet rope around his own neck. I only obliged him by kicking the chair out from under him and ending his sorry life.''

She couldn't believe he was admitting it to her, to a cop. ''You did that yourself?'' she asked stiffly.

''Vargas was stupid enough to try to blackmail me!'' Frank was angry now and yelling over the explosion of a bottle rocket coming from the alley. ''The little squealer couldn't be trusted to keep what he knew to himself. And he was seeing O'Rourke, spilling his guts to the man like he did in the old days in the confessional!''

So why was he admitting all this? Did he really think she would keep it all in the family?

"Is that why you framed Dermot? Because you thought he knew something about you?"

"That and because he interfered in my business."

"How?"

"He tried to save you."

Stella felt as if the air was knocked out of her. She realized he was talking about the rape.

His business, he'd said.

"You ordered Rick Lamey to rape me?"

"No, of course not. I didn't want you hurt, Star. I just wanted you scared so you would keep your mouth shut. It never occurred to me that I needed to spell it out for them."

"I don't understand."

"I ran the Vipers. I got the info for the burglaries. You know how people talk to their favorite mechanic? When they're not gonna be home a particular night. Or when they're getting the car ready for vacation. The Vipers pulled off the jobs under my direction. Then I fenced the product and gave them a better cut than they could have gotten on the street. And they brought me as many vehicles as they could lift off the street. A chop shop can be a *very* lucrative business."

Leroy's comment about not liking the way Frank did business came back to her. All along, the family patriarch had been running a chop shop. And he'd used part of that money to help support her and her mom and sister. Stella felt shame for him. Shame he obviously would never experience himself.

Wondering if the mechanic who'd come into the

store the day before had been looking for hot parts—
that had to be why Frank had made it a point to in-
troduce her as his cousin the detective—she said, "I
don't know you anymore. I wonder if I ever did. I
thought you cared about us."

"I did care. I care now. But you're no good to me.
You would betray me faster than Tony did. At one
time I thought of Tony as the son I never had. He
worked in the store doing odd jobs for cash. And he
was the kid who went through windows to open doors
for the bigger boys. I took him up to Wisconsin more
than once. Treated him like my own. And see how
he repaid me? You're no better."

"I'm a cop, Frank."

"And I'm the power in this neighborhood! You
made a mistake crossing me!"

Aghast, Stella stared at the man who'd been like a
father to her. He looked the same on the outside, but
she realized what was on the inside was rotten to the
core. She realized he always had been rotten inside,
only she'd been too young and naive to recognize
that.

Frank attached himself to people only for as long
as they were useful in some way. Like a pretend family. *Her* family. Then once their usefulness was over,
he didn't care what happened to them. He'd acted hurt
that she hadn't been to see him much over the past
few years, when the truth was he hadn't done anything to see her, either. All an act.

"You run the neighborhood like you ran our family?" she asked, trying to stay calm. "You pretended
to care for us, then turned around and gave orders for
a heinous crime to be committed against me. What in

the world have you done to the people around here?''
she asked, seeing a few neighbors watching from the
safety of their doorways.

He ignored the last. ''I told them bastards to scare
you, not hurt you! I just wanted your promise of silence! I didn't want to hurt you this time, either,
Star—''

''Don't call me that!''

''—but you wouldn't settle down and quit. You
had to stick your nose where it didn't belong again!''

''So when you couldn't discourage me, you decided to hand out your own brand of justice.'' Stella
blinked and saw the gun in Frank's hand. She backed
up and cursed herself for not being prepared for this.
''*You* ordered Paz Falco to kill me.''

''You gave me no choice! But he couldn't get it
right. If I want things done right, sometimes I just
have to do them myself.'' More firecrackers banged
behind him, making him raise his voice so she imagined the whole neighborhood could hear him. ''*You*
should have died tonight, Star, not Falco!''

So he hadn't stuck around long enough to know
the man wasn't dead. At least she hoped not.

And then the thought struck her. ''My God, you
were trying to kill *me?*''

''I missed and got him instead. But I won't miss
again, not at this short distance.''

To Stella's horror, the man she'd thought of as a
father aimed and pulled the trigger.

She saw the blue flash, felt her chest crush and flew
back against a car hood. She gasped and tried to
speak, but she couldn't get any air. She tried to reach
for her holster but couldn't manage it.

She couldn't move anything.

"You made me kill you, Star. Remember that."

Frank turned his back on her and left her to die alone.

Chapter Fifteen

Spotting the Frank's Auto Repair sign, Dermot instinctively slowed the vehicle in time to see the man who must be Frank Jacobek raise a gun and shoot Stella. Slamming on the brakes, he jumped out of the SUV and saw her sprawl back over a car hood. Still armed, her cousin had turned his back on her.

Dermot thought fast.

Praying Stella was still alive, he knew he had to get the gun first, *then* see to her. If he tried to help her first, Frank could simply kill them both.

Under the cover of nearby fireworks, Dermot crept toward the lot, his focus Frank, who got to a Jaguar with an open trunk before glancing back. The armed man stiffened, and his expression turned horrified.

Dermot slid behind a tree and followed the older man's gaze.

Stella was gone!

Relieved that she was alive, worried that she was seriously hurt, Dermot was torn about what to do next.

Frank decided for him. He muttered a curse, grabbed a rifle from the Jaguar trunk and slammed the lid shut. Then he stalked off toward the alley where his neighbors were putting on a fireworks display. He didn't even bother to hide the two weapons in his hands.

And Dermot didn't wait until the man disappeared from view.

Knowing he had to take Frank as quickly as possible, Dermot broke cover and jogged across the lot. When he got to the edge of the building, he slowed just long enough to see where Frank had gone. Seemingly beside himself—Stella was nowhere in view—Frank was waving the rifle at the families who were holding their Day of the Dead fireworks display in the alley.

"Where's Stella?" Frank demanded.

Mothers gathered their children close and retreated into their yards away from the madman. Most of the men stood in mute defiance.

"You keep her from me and you know what you'll get!" Frank yelled.

The handful of people who refused to leave the alley remained steely-eyed and continued to shoot off their illegal fireworks. A teenager lit a bottle rocket, but it fizzled out and did nothing. He flapped around it, frustrated that it was too dangerous to touch.

Almost as dangerous as Frank Jacobek, Dermot thought.

Dermot slid closer. A lone woman beyond the bastard looked straight at Dermot…then at Frank…then back to him. She nodded, then made a small gesture toward her gate.

Stella? he silently mouthed.

Another nod.

The knot in the middle of his chest eased a bit. These people were protecting her.

"Stella!" Frank yelled, then pointed his rifle at the teenager who was still trying to decide what to do about his dud of a bottle rocket. "Where the hell is she?"

"I don't know, man!"

"She came this way!" Spittle sprayed from Frank's mouth. "She couldn't have just disappeared. You're lying! One of you is hiding her!"

Then Dermot was on Frank and kicked him in the back of his knee so hard that he collapsed to one side. The rifle hit the pavement and went spinning out of Frank's reach. He was agile, though, and whirled around, handgun raised.

"O'Rourke! I should have killed you, too!"

Dermot didn't wait until Frank finished—another well-placed kick and that weapon went flying.

Frank was on his feet in a flash and came after Dermot with his bare hands. No matter that he had an extra twenty years on Dermot, he was solid, tough and mean. He pummeled Dermot's middle with both fists. Dermot struck back with a blow to Frank's jaw that didn't seem to faze him. Neither did the second or third blow. The man simply kept coming.

Frank moved fast and grabbed a black plastic garbage container and sent it skidding into Dermot. Then he went after the fallen gun that lay a few yards away.

"I wouldn't if I were you, Frank!" came an authoritative woman's voice.

"Stella!"

Dermot glanced back to see her standing outside that woman's gate, one hip resting heavily against another garbage container, Frank's rifle in her hands and pointed straight at him.

"Everyone get back!" she said.

They obeyed, retreating behind fences or in pockets at the side of the alley.

Dermot quickly scanned Stella for blood, but couldn't see any. Then he quickly turned his attention once more to Frank, who was very slowly backing down the alley away from her. As if he had anywhere to go where the arm of the law wouldn't reach him.

"Frank, stop now!"

"You wouldn't shoot me, Star."

"Don't make me. Frank Jacobek, you're under arrest. Put your hands in the air!"

While he didn't try for the gun, neither did he do as she ordered. He kept inching backward.

Stella tried to move toward him, but she grimaced with the pain. It took everything Dermot had not to go to her to help her. She was a cop. This was her bust. She would be humiliated if he stepped in now. He had to let her handle it, had to let her work through the pain. She could do it—he knew she could do anything she set her mind to.

"You have a right to remain silent, Frank. Anything you say can be used against you in a court of law." Stella ground out his Miranda rights. "You have a right to an attorney. If you cannot afford—"

"Shut your trap, girl!" Frank shouted. "Don't you know you'll never best me?"

He started to move off.

"Frank, stop!"

He didn't so much as look back.

"Frank, if you don't stop and let me cuff you," Stella said, moving after him with difficulty, "I really will have to shoot you."

He made a rude gesture and kept going.

Stella stopped, lowered the rifle barrel and shot him in the leg.

Frank screamed, "Bitch!" and nearly went down right there.

Just then, as he was dancing to stay on his feet, someone threw a string of firecrackers into the alley behind him. Frank jerked in surprise, then stepped wrong. His foot jammed against the unexploded bottle rocket. He cursed and kicked it to get it out of the way.

The jarring awakened the faulty rocket, and as it went spinning, suddenly flared to life. Frank couldn't move out of the way fast enough. The rocket shot up into his groin, and then Frank flared to life, too, screaming as his whole body was engulfed in flames.

"Frank, no!" Stella yelled, dropping the rifle and trying to get to him. "Water! Someone get a hose!"

No one moved to help. His neighbors looked on him with hatred and a sense of satisfaction that was tangible to Dermot. One old lady spat in his direction.

Frank threw himself down to the alley floor and rolled, but nothing could save him now. His skin was blackening and separating from his body, and his jerky movements were slowing.

Dermot grabbed Stella before she incinerated herself trying to help someone who was beyond help. He let her sob against him, knowing it was probably the last time he would ever hold her in his arms.

He turned her away from the ghastly sight.

The puppet master of the neighborhood was no more.

"NOW I CAN SAY, yes, it's worth making Kevlar a fashion statement," Stella joked with Logan, who had grilled her while medical personnel had come in and out of the emergency room cubicle.

Not that she had any cause for amusement, having watched Frank die such a horrible death only hours before. Because of her. Because she'd shot him in the leg and he hadn't been able to move out of the way fast enough.

She couldn't believe he'd tried to kill her. Only her Kevlar vest had saved her. And even at that, she'd almost been knocked out cold. She had lots of bruising and a fractured rib, but in a few weeks, the doctor had said, she would be as good as new.

Rather, her body would be.

Her heart was a different matter.

Dermot had called 9-1-1, had followed the ambulance to the emergency room.

Then he had disappeared.

And while she'd been poked and prodded, she'd used that time to think.

"I need to find Dermot," she told Logan, trying to sit up so she could swing her legs over the edge of the bed.

"Whoa, whoa, whoa." Logan stopped her from going further. "You haven't been released yet. Besides, you have—I can't tell you how much—paperwork to fill out on this case."

Logan was right, of course. Dermot would have to wait.

And then she realized she was being foolish torturing herself over him. Dermot hadn't waited, had he? Why should he when she'd told him she wouldn't forgive him?

And yet, that hadn't stopped him from following her to Frank's place. To her rescue one more time...

Why had he?

She was trying to get up again when she heard a deep voice ask, "Need some help?"

Her pulse began to thunder, "Yeah. A little."

Dermot—not Logan—was standing over her bed.

She swung her legs out, and he helped her slide forward so she was sitting on the edge. Any movement of her torso was still difficult—the painkiller was wearing off—but it was worth it to feel his hands on her, if only for a moment.

His expression neutral, Dermot backed off. "Logan said you needed to find me."

"I wanted to thank you—"

"I don't want your thanks, Star. In the end I really didn't do anything. You got Falco and Frank...well, Frank was served justice by a higher court."

He sounded so matter-of-fact, as if he'd seen it all in a movie or something, rather than being involved.

She said, "That's one way of putting it, I guess."

"His death was not your fault."

Stella nodded. "I'll try to see it that way." And then she met his gaze. "You were there for me, Dermot. But by letting me handle the situation, you showed you trusted me." That he didn't see her as a victim anymore. "I didn't do that for you. Trust, I mean."

"You've done something great for me that I

couldn't do for myself. The charges against me are being dropped.''

Stella heaved a sigh of relief and let her chin drop to her chest. "Thank goodness."

There was an awkward pause between them for a moment before Dermot asked, "So how are you really?''

"Physically? A mess." *Emotionally? A train wreck.*

"I'm sorry."

"Don't apologize. You didn't do anything that needs to be forgiven."

Dermot gave her a sharp look. "Star…you want to explain that in a little more detail?''

"I love the way you say my name." She swallowed hard and steeled herself for possible rejection. Putting herself in the line of fire of a gun was small potatoes compared to this. "I love *you,* Dermot."

"Even though you know the truth."

"*Because* I know the truth," she said.

She waited a moment but he didn't return the sentiment. Her nerves felt raw. Was he simply disappointed in her and angry? Or had what happened between them changed the way he felt about her forever?

"I was thinking the other day that I never really knew the real you until now." She had to try to explain, even if it didn't make a difference to him. "Twelve years ago, I loved you because you saved me. I had a glorified vision of who you were. Now I love you for so much more. For who you were before that. For the person you made yourself into. For your humanity and kindness and strength. Now I know everything, Dermot…well…other than those things you can't talk about…and my heart is filled with you.''

He shook his head. ''But the seal—''

''Is part of who you are.'' Getting to her feet, she moved closer and touched his face. ''An honorable man. That's why there's nothing to forgive and why I couldn't ask for more.''

Dermot smiled down at her then, and she thought his was the most beautiful smile in the world. ''I couldn't ask for more, either, Star. I love you and I always will.''

He put his arms around her and held her protectively, and Stella decided she liked the feeling just fine. She sighed and snuggled closer.

Dermot brushed his lips against her forehead, her nose, her lips. His kiss was sweet and lingering and joyful. Exactly the way she was feeling.

''Can you really forget the past, then, and build a future with me?'' Dermot asked.

His sweet words made her heart sing and erased all the heartache of the past. ''I can't think of anything I want more.''

Epilogue

"Another job well done," Gideon said, sitting on the edge of his desk.

Dermot O'Rourke was a free man...well, except for his attachment to Stella Jacobek.

He passed the newspaper he'd been reading so Gabe and Blade and Cass could take a look at the article commending Detective Stella Jacobek for making the key arrest in the Vargas case and cracking a chop shop and burglary ring.

"We didn't do a whole lot to help Dermot," Gabe said. "Stella didn't really need us."

"Don't sell yourself short," Cass said. "You found the key to eliminating Marta Ortiz. And the link between Tony Vargas and Frank Jacobek."

"But Stella's the one who nailed it."

Blade said, "Stella turned out to be one fine detective." And he couldn't sound prouder of his old friend.

"Indeed she did," Gideon agreed, thinking they'd have use for her skills in the future.

Who knew when their next case would come along....

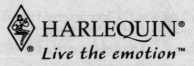

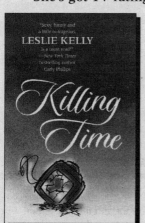

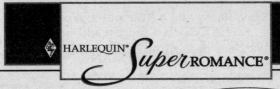
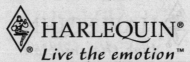

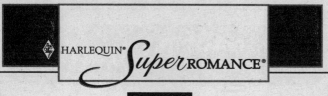

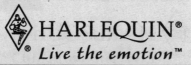

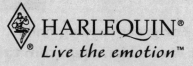

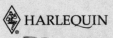
INTRIGUE

COMING NEXT MONTH

#789 BULLETPROOF BILLIONAIRE by Mallory Kane
New Orleans Confidential
New Orleans Confidential agent Seth Lewis took on the alias of a suave international tycoon to infiltrate the Cajun Mob. He'd set out to gain entry by charming the rich widow Adrienne DeBlanc into telling him everything. It wasn't long before his protective instincts surfaced for the fragile beauty, but could he risk a high-stakes case for love?

#790 MIDNIGHT DISCLOSURES by Rita Herron
Nighthawk Island
In one tragic moment, radio psychologist Dr. Claire Kos had lost everything. She survived, only to become a serial killer's next target. Blind and vulnerable to attack, she turned to FBI agent Mark Steele—the man she'd loved and lost. As the killer took aim, Mark was poised to protect the woman he couldn't live without.

#791 ON THE LIST by Patricia Rosemoor
Club Undercover
Someone wanted to silence agent Renata Fox for good. She knew the Feds had accused the wrong person of being the Chicago sniper, but her speculations had somehow landed her on the real killer's hit list. So when Gabriel Connor showed up claiming he was on the assassin's trail, Renata knew she had to put her life—and her heart—in Gabe's hands....

#792 A DANGEROUS INHERITANCE by Leona Karr
Eclipse
When a storm delivered heiress Stacy Ashford into the iron-hard embrace of Josh Spencer, it seemed their meeting was fated. Gaining her inheritance depended on reopening the eerie hotel where Josh's kid sister died. And even though Stacy's inheritance bound them to an ever-tightening coil of danger, would Josh's oath to avenge his sister cost him the one woman who truly mattered?

#793 INTENSIVE CARE by Jessica Andersen
When Dr. Ripley Davis saw another of her patients flatline, she knew someone was killing the people in her care. But before she could find the real murderer, overbearing, impossibly sexy police officer Zachary Cage accused her of the crime. It wasn't long before her fiery resolve convinced him she wasn't the prime suspect...she was the prime *target*.

#794 SUDDEN ALLIANCE by Jackie Manning
When undercover operative Liam O'Shea found Sarah Regis on the side of the road, battered and incoherent, his razor-sharp instincts warned him she was in danger. As an amnesic murder witness, her only hope for survival was to stay in close proximity to Liam. Would their sudden alliance survive the secrets she'd kept locked inside?

www.eHarlequin.com

HICNM0704